SURPRISE MATES

INTERSTELLAR BRIDES® PROGRAM: BOOK 21

GRACE GOODWIN

GET A FREE BOOK!

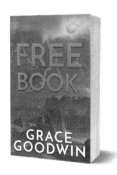

FIND YOUR INTERSTELLAR MATCH!

YOUR mate is out there. Take the test today and discover your perfect match. Are you ready for a sexy alien mate (or two)?

VOLUNTEER NOW!

interstellarbridesprogram.com

ucy, Transport Station 345, Prillon Prime

"WHAT HAPPENS ON PRILLON PRIME—"

The sizzle and hair-raising hum of transport cut off Rachel's words. One second we were on The Colony, looking down from the raised platform at CJ and Rezzer, each holding one of their twins; the next I'm looking at some seriously burly Prillons manning the controls on Prillon Prime.

"—stays on Prillon Prime," Rachel finished as if we hadn't just traveled like people on *Star Trek* or the wizards in *Harry Potter*, minus the flushing toilet.

"Mate, what are you suggesting?" Maxim said, taking Rachel's hand and leading her down the steps. His second, Ryston, followed closely behind. Rachel, meanwhile, held their sleepy son in her arms. He was half

Prillon and big for his age. Rachel's biceps were working overtime, but she shook her head when Ryston reached for the boy.

Cute.

Rachel leaned around Ryston and glanced at me. Gave me a wink to go along with her grin.

"I saw that," Kiel stated plainly. He stilled his own mate with a hand upon her shoulder.

Lindsey looked up at her Everian hottie. "What?"

"What?" he repeated. "Whenever you all get together, I get scared."

Lindsey laughed. "You, scared?"

I bit my cheek because the three big aliens were staring my way. I was the unmated one of this group, pretty much the fifth—make that sixth—wheel for the entire party.

The Everian Hunter leaned down and kissed the top of his mate's head.

Meanwhile Rachel pressed her lips to Max's dark hair. The little boy slept in his mother's arms. Pushing two, he was too little to stay behind like the older boy, Lindsey's and Kiel's son, Wyatt, so Max was joining a few other little ones at the party. It worked out well because Wyatt was best buddies with Tanner and Emma, who were more eager to stay on The Colony with their new Atlan uncles Braun, Kai and the rest of them, acting like walking jungle gyms anytime the little ones were around.

"You and Wyatt are the only ones who can destroy me," Kiel murmured.

Lindsey's face took on that sappy, lovey-dovey look.

"Oh, Kiel," she whispered, then sniffed and lifted her

chin. "We've come for a surprise birthday party." Her words were the reminder for all of us as to why we were here. "What kind of trouble could we possibly get into?"

Kiel's eyes went wide, and he slowly shook his head as if the possibilities were endless.

"This is why the Prime and every male in attendance agreed it had to happen within the walls of the palace."

"Palace," Rachel humphed. "More like a fortress."

"Exactly," the three males said at the exact same time.

The hum of the transport pad had us stepping off it so the second transport from The Colony could arrive.

"This is the reason we didn't let you ladies transport without us," Maxim said as we stood in the large room and waited.

The space was twice as big as the transport room on The Colony, and I had to assume it was kept busy. I'd never been to Prillon Prime before. Heck, I'd never been anywhere else in space but where Olivia and Wulf were stationed. My BFF and her hulking Atlan mate were the reason why I wasn't on Earth, not because I'd been matched. I was, in fact, one of very few humans out in Coalition space who were single and not fighting the Hive. At least that's what I'd been told. As in, the only single lady. Fighters didn't count.

Now I was going to the Prime's palace for a surprise birthday party for his mate, Jessica, another human. This was epically big.

Epic.

Even more so than a girls' weekend in Vegas. This was Prillon Prime, baby!

I'd never met Prime Nial, or the birthday girl for that

matter, but I'd chatted with them, along with Jessica's second mate, Ander, on a phone call. Or screen-to-screen call. Phones were beyond old-fashioned, like a horse and buggy, for these guys.

I had to catch up on space terminology. Without a mate to help me adjust to my new life, I was getting behind.

Not that I didn't have mate offers on The Colony. The Atlan Warlord Braun was an absolute sweetheart, a great big freaking teddy bear... and I didn't want him. Not like that. Same with Captain Marz and his Prillon second. Same with the other Atlans. The Viken fighters. The large selection of available mates on The Colony was, frankly, overwhelming.

Worse, not one of them felt right, as if I wanted one to be *mine*. Braun was, if nothing else, my friend. I trusted him and I liked him, but I didn't want to take off all my clothes and rub my naked body over his.

Not even a little. Which was just sad because he was hot. Like sex-on-a-stick hot. But my indifference was also the reason my guardian, Warlord Wulf, gave every male on The Colony the hands-off vibe when it came to me.

The truth was, I was on The Colony to be with Olivia, Tanner and Emma. They were my family. Not by blood but by choice. Either way, I didn't want another one. Not yet. I wasn't ready. If I hooked up with any of the honorable warriors on The Colony, they would want forever. Like, forever-forever, and mating and babies and the whole thing. And that was a large commitment. Gigantic.

These next few days, I just wanted to have some fun. Maybe have some hot sex with a virile alien or two, take the edge off, and get back to my de facto niece and nephew and my best friend. I was happy there. Mostly. Bored sometimes but content. I didn't want anything to ruin my new life.

I'd had no one on Earth. No family. Few friends. A low-paying job where I was invisible most of the time. Only Olivia and her kids mattered to me. Without them, I would be alone and, worse, lonely as hell. To Tanner and Emma, I was *Aunt Woocy*, and nothing mattered more to me than making sure those babies were happy and healthy.

I wasn't enough of a selfish bitch to use any of the warriors on the colony just for sex. Those guys had been through so much. Battle. Capture. Torture. Integration. Rejection from their home worlds. I was not going to play with them like that. To have some fun, I would have to go off world—like here on Prillon Prime—and make sure whoever I had some fun with knew that's all it was. Fun. Temporary.

Luckily the women from The Colony were all super nice and cool enough to want me to join them. I had a feeling Lindsey would have had T-shirts made that said *Earth Girls Unite* if she could. Since she'd been a PR rep on Earth and was still going at it, working on trying to bring new Earth volunteers to the Brides program *and* planning a huge surprise party for her BFF, *the* Lady Jessica Deston, the freaking *queen* of the entire Interstellar Coalition of Planets. Safe to say, Lindsey had probably been a little distracted.

"We ladies are perfectly capable of transporting by ourselves," Rachel said, patting Maxim's arm. Then she smiled. "But I like it when you get all protective and growly."

Both he and Ryston growled to match her words. I bit my lip, trying not to laugh. Every male I'd encountered in space was bossier than the next. Protective. Dominant. All alpha-male hotness. Wulf was that way with Olivia and the kids, but he was also that way with me. He was like the brother I'd never had. If a girl from Ohio could have a seven-foot-plus Atlan beast as a brother. An overprotective, growly, beat-the-pulp-out-of-anyone-interested-in-getting-in-my-pants big brother.

"There is no chance you will transport without us. You would probably transport to Viken's Trixon Resort," Maxim grumbled.

"What's that?" I asked.

"A retreat for new mates to *get to know each other.*" Rachel made little air quotes with her fingers. "It's hedonistic. Think tropical five-star resort that caters to every sexual desire."

I got hot at the thought. Who wouldn't want that? "Like a spa but with sex?"

Maxim was the one who nodded. "Exactly."

Rachel went up on her tiptoes and kissed his square jaw. "I've talked to Whitney, you know. She told me that place is only fun if your mates are with you. Not that I don't enjoy a little *solo* fun."

Maxim's body went rigid as his gaze met his mate's.

"Don't tease us, mate," Ryston growled. "We don't have time to watch you at this moment. We are due at the palace."

Rachel's cheeks flushed as red as my hair, and she

finally surrendered her son to Ryston, who cuddled the sleepy toddler close to his chest.

Cuteness overload.

I could tell Rachel was equally embarrassed and aroused by Ryston calling her out. I was jealous. So jealous. Body and heart aching with longing. I wanted a guy or two who'd get hot about watching me flick the bean. Hell, I wanted a guy or two just to *look* at me without staring at me like I was going to save their eternal soul and grant them new life. I wanted sexy fun—without Wulf glaring at every male in sight like he might dismember them if they stepped in my direction.

I was distracted from my thoughts by the gorgeous queen of Viken, who walked by. I couldn't help but stare. Yeah, I knew who she was by her red hair and her dress —I'd been a stylist on Earth and knew fashion, even in space—and the fact that she had three hot, almost identical guys with her. She passed with her hot kings flanking her on a side as protection, and each one with a menacing and heated look that made me squirm. I had to wonder if they'd been to that sex spa place on Viken. Trixon Resort. That was going in the mental file for later.

Shit. I was in trouble here. Sex-on-the-brain twenty-four-seven kind of trouble.

Or was that twenty-six hours, forty-two or whatever the hell kind of calendar they had on this crazy planet? I had no idea. All I knew was I hadn't been with a guy in way too long, and my body was hungry for some attention like the shape-shifters I'd read about in some of my favorite romance novels. *Touch hungry*, they called it.

When need and ache grew to the point where one couldn't think straight. Maybe I had Atlan fever.

Yeah. That was me, thinking I had *Atlan fever.* God. Every second on Prillon Prime was making me worse. Talk about a full-on hot-alpha-male buffet, and I hadn't even made it out of the transport room. The thought of Prillon warriors walking around in pairs all over the place? Oh fuck, yes.

I'll take two to go, please.

Once Wulf heard I wasn't seeking commitment in a relationship, he'd taken my wishes to heart. He'd put out a memo that I was off-limits, taking the big-brother role to the extreme. I might as well have had a poisonous vagina or something.

That was why Rachel, Kristin, Lindsey, Olivia, Caroline and Mikki all told me I had to get some action while I was on Prillon Prime. They agreed The Colony guys were off-limits, but this was a different planet. A short-term visit. A two-day fling! Party time!

I totally agreed and had spent the last few days working the S-Gen machine to make some super-hot and sexy lingerie. No male, alien or human, could resist lace, satin and barely covered nipples and pussy.

Yeah, here I was. Unmated, horny girl on vacation in space. Hopeful to get a few male-induced orgasms on Prillon Prime, especially since Wulf wasn't going to be here to cockblock. He and Olivia were stuck on Earth doing PR interviews for the *Bachelor Beast* program. While they were doing the talk-show circuit light-years away, I was going to do a Prillon Prime circuit of my own.

That was the plan, anyway. First I had to find a worthy candidate, then convince him—or them—to sex me up.

With all the testosterone—did aliens have testosterone?—walking around, I doubted it'd be too difficult. I wasn't a supermodel, but I wasn't unfortunate looking either. When I'd been a kid, my pops had called me his little leprechaun thanks to my mop of red hair and bright green eyes. Now I had freckles galore and a nose ring to go with it, so hopefully I looked like the gold at the end of the rainbow and not an ugly duckling.

But I'd never seen a Prillon woman—female alien—whatever. I had no idea what I was competing with here. As far as I knew, I was the only human female in the group who didn't already have a mate. So I wasn't planning on competing with my friends, just the locals.

"Be mindful and cautious, Lucy. Our intel states Cerberus is still seeking a human female for his own," Maxim said, and everyone once again looked at me.

Those words were like being shoved into a freezing cold shower. Cerberus wasn't stupid enough to take an already claimed woman. He might be the Wicked Witch of the West of space, but he wasn't dumb. He wanted an unmated human. One nobody'd go after.

That would be... me.

I raised a hand to stop Maxim from continuing on the topic, which was a total Debbie Downer. "I have no intention of doing anything crazy. I promise to stay inside the palace at all times."

Maxim, Ryston, and Kiel stared at me skeptically while the ladies smirked, but I spoke the truth. I had no interest in being Cerberus's side piece. The idea made me ill. I'd take the guards Maxim or any of the guys decided to assign me. I was fine with being safe. If the guards were hot and could fuck me against a wall or on any horizontal surface in the palace while watching over me, I'd be totally satisfied.

Oh yes, I would, and I was sure more than once.

Caroline, Rezzer, and little CJ and RJ arrived on the transport platform we'd just vacated, and I waved to the twins. It was still weird to have them magically appear from one second to the next. They came down off the platform, and the twins clapped with excitement, then wiggled to be free. At not yet two years old, they were eager to explore. Younger than Tanner and Emma, they weren't quite ready to be separated from their parents. Or their parents weren't quite ready to be separated from them. They'd spent many hours at playdates with Tanner and Emma, as had all the children. They all called me Aunt Woocy, too. It was too damn adorable. They loved me, and I loved them back.

It should be enough. So why did I feel empty?

"Why is everyone staring at Lucy?" Rezzer asked, leaning to let CJ down. She ran off like a streak and right for the transport controls. Rezzer dashed after and scooped her right back up. She fussed but he gave her a zerbert and she giggled. "Can we get to the palace before this one sets the controls and sends us all to Sector Zero?"

With Maxim in the lead, we exited the transport room. The ladies hung back with me, but the guys looked over their shoulders to make sure we followed.

"This is going to be the best time ever," Lindsey said. "But we need to hurry. The surprise party is supposed to start in three hours. That's not very much time to get ready."

Caroline nodded and I saw that little RJ's eyes were drooping, his head on her shoulder. Transport was exhausting, and his small body was probably ready for nap time. His sister—she was a pistol and would probably run until she tipped over—was climbing over Rezzer's shoulders so she could see better. "I'm so glad you organized babysitters. A party with fancy dresses and Lucy's gorgeous makeup work..."

"Yeah, I'm going to feel like a princess," Rachel added. "You really need to set up a spa, Lucy."

I laughed. "On The Colony? All the guys are grumps, and there aren't enough ladies."

"Maybe a retreat like the Trixon Resort," Rachel countered, wiggling her eyebrows. "Whitney told me they even have sexual instructors there in case you want to try some new things and aren't sure how to—you know—get started." Her guilty giggle was contagious, and soon every one of us ladies was grinning.

"You're obsessed, mate," Maxim replied. "We didn't satisfy you enough this morning?"

Rachel flushed. "I'm thinking of a business for Lucy," she countered. "It would be a hit."

"Lucy's right. Not on The Colony. Maybe Prillon Prime," Maxim said, making me wonder what the planet was like. "The females here enjoy pampering."

"I think you'd be surprised what a nice massage could do for a grumpy warrior," Rachel insisted.

"We are willing to allow you to demonstrate, mate." Ryston's suggestion was filled with heat. She laughed.

"We'd never get that far."

Maxim leaned in and lifted Rachel's face to his for a kiss. "As for feeling like a princess, mate, Jessica is an actual royal, and you are the wonderful Lady Rone of The Colony." Maxim gave her a very heated look, and I had to wonder who hadn't gotten enough this morning.

I was just Lucy Vandermark. Mateless but with sexy underwear.

Lindsey smiled. "I for one am looking forward to dressing up and having some adult time. Tonight we have the big surprise party, brunch with the ladies tomorrow, a full day of lounging around and relaxing, and then, day three, an actual *royal ball*. Huge dresses. Music from home. Dancing. Earth food for days. Girlfriends to talk to. We might never want to leave."

Kiel scowled and Maxim growled. "You will return with us to The Colony," Maxim commanded Rachel.

"She's teasing you boys." After Rachel gave Maxim an air-kiss, she flung her arm around my shoulder. "Let's get the party started. Because... what happens on Prillon Prime..."

"Stays on Prillon Prime!" All of us finished the sentence together, giving me hope that I might find a hot guy willing to spend this weekend peeling off my undies with his teeth.

The guys turned to look at us with our shouting.

Yeah, this was going to be fun.

mbassador Lord Niklas Lorvar, Prillon Prime, The Palace

"SURPRISE!"

Queen Jessica, with her mates behind her—Prime Nial and Lord Ander—stopped dead in her tracks as she came into the ballroom, her eyes widening like dinner plates and her mouth dropping open. Once the initial shock was over, she covered her face with her hands and laughed. Male clapping joined squeals of feminine laughter and shouting as a clutch of human women surrounded her like Hive on a downed fighter.

"Stop scowling, Niklas," Sambor scolded while he, too, clapped slowly, his rough hands coming together like slow-moving thunder.

I watched the stunned happiness on the queen's face as she realized many of her fellow Earth brides had come from their home planets to Prillon Prime to celebrate her birthing day. I'd heard one of the females had organized it with the queen's mates, obviously having kept it all a secret. We'd received an invitation, something I knew, as ambassador, not to decline.

My duties to Prillon Prime were of the utmost importance to the entire Coalition Fleet. And part of my job was to maintain an excellent working relationship with both Prime Nial and his second, Lord Ander.

Turning down an invitation to their mate's private celebration was not an option—no matter what pressing matters awaited mine and Sambor's attention. Criminal activities on Rogue 5. Cerberus Legion's new interest in human females. Dr. Helion and the Intelligence Core's attempts to extract information from a Nexus unit we were holding in captivity. Important things for the safety and security of everyone present, and everyone in the Interstellar Coalition of Planets. Instead of taking care of these issues, I was supposed to remain here for several days, sneaking away for meetings, only to return for more celebrations, which I'd been informed were to include a sweet baked item from Earth called *cake* and listening to strange Earthen music for hours upon hours. I had never listened to human music, but knowing how chaotic and unpredictable humans were as a whole, I did not have high hopes that their music would be tolerable to Prillon ears.

"We should not be here, Sambor. There is too much work to do."

"We already must transport off planet for meetings twice during the celebration days." Sambor still clapped his large hands, and he had a smile on his face. "That's more than enough. What's the point of fighting all the time if we don't enjoy ourselves once in a while?"

"The custom of shocking one on their birthing day does not qualify as a worthy use of our time. We should be out in the field protecting the queen, not standing here watching her cry." For the female was crying profusely, and every female who approached and hugged her seemed to make the crying worse. "Perhaps the females from Earth are not as intelligent as I had assumed. Why do they not stop?" I could not stand to see a female in pain, as was the case with most of the males in the room. I expected Ander and Nial to be severely affected, emotionally linked to the queen as they were through their dark red mating collars, but they beamed like they'd just won a fierce battle. "I do not understand females."

Sambor burst into laughter. "A truer statement has never passed your lips, my friend."

I wasn't one for surprises and it wasn't a Prillon tradition to make a celebration a secret, but it appeared to be something normal for the primitive planet where all the squealing females were from. And something they clearly enjoyed.

"Niklas, no jest. Stop scowling. You're going to give Prime Nial the impression you don't want to be here," Sambor continued, although the Prime was far too enthralled by his mate's joyful face to note the frown on mine.

"I'm too busy." Right then, music came through hidden speakers and I cringed. I'd never heard such a theme before, but all the females squealed again and laughed. They grabbed one another by the hands and dragged each other toward an open area I assumed was designated for dancing.

However, the strange high-pitched male voice coming through the speakers had the ladies twirling, gyrating, stomping and waving their hands all around in the oddest type of ceremonial display I'd ever witnessed.

Ah, Earth music. Loud, odd and weirdly rhythmic. As I had feared.

I listened to the words. "Why do they want to spin a baby right round? And what is a record? Is that what is wrong with humans, that they were spun in circles as infants?"

Next to me, Sambor looked as confused as I felt, and shrugged. "Why are their motions not in sync?"

I wondered the same. "Perhaps they have not properly learned the steps." Every female, beautiful in her own right—some wearing Prillon collars, others Trion adornments, some with Atlan mating cuffs about their wrists—was moving as if distinctly separate from the others.

"They look like flapping birds panicked by a serpent." Sambor's dry humor was one of the reasons I kept him around all these years. The smile that creased my face was true.

"So they do. Lovely birds." I did not allow my gaze to linger overlong on any one female, despite the beauty on display before us, as their very possessive mates watched from every angle and corner of the room. Sambor and I were one of less than a dozen unmated males who had been trusted to attend. I would not insult our Prime by causing problems with any of the mated females.

Nor did I wish to battle a raging Atlan beast or pair of mated Prillon males who might take offense at my interest in their mate.

"Why do they threaten endless spinning of their infants?" he asked, wincing. "'Baby' is their word for infant, correct? My NPU is not malfunctioning?"

"If so, mine is as well." I noticed expressions similar to Sambor's on the other males about the room. That had the corner of my lips tipping up yet again. I wasn't the only one suffering. The ladies clapped in time to the heavy beats of music with obvious delight.

A beautiful young female moved to the front of the room and took a comm from the technician operating the strange, human music system. She lifted the unit to her mouth as the music faded. Thank the gods.

"Hi, everyone! I'm Lindsey from The Colony. That sexy Hunter, Kiel, is my mate." She waved, her gaze lit with mischief. "Hi, sexy!"

Sambor and I turned our heads to see a large, very intimidating male standing with his arms crossed and an amused expression on his face as he lifted his fingers in the smallest possible wave. It was enough. Lindsey blew him a kiss and Sambor chuckled.

"Lucky fucker."

"Indeed." The Hunter would have been intimidating if not for this odd festive occasion. We had worked with Elite Hunter squads many times. Never did they look so... harmless.

Lindsey continued, moving her fingers now to indicate that Queen Jessica should come to the front. I returned my attention to the gathering of the other females, twittering with anticipation as the queen came forward to stand next to Lindsey.

"Happy birthday, Jessica!" Lindsey wrapped an arm around the queen and gave her an odd side hug.

The ladies all shouted the same as the shocked males looked on. We would not dare refer to her so familiarly.

The queen beamed. "Thank you all so much for this amazing surprise. Thank you, Lindsey. I know you helped Nial and Ander do this for me. I love you so much." She looked up, tears gathering in her eyes as she worshipped her mates with her gaze. Never had she been shy about claiming her males in public—from the very first in the combat arena where she'd claimed both Nial and Ander before the entire crowd—and that was one of the reasons she was so beloved by all Prillons.

Fuck that. The entire Coalition Fleet.

The queen and Lindsey shared a look and Sambor chuckled. "I know females, Nik. That looks like trouble."

I had to agree, but I remained silent as the queen continued.

"Do you know what I want for my birthday, ladies?"

"What?" a bunch of them shouted.

"Line dancing!"

The females put their hands in the air, their screams nearly deafening every suffering male in the room.

"What the fuck is a line dance?" Sambor asked.

"I have no idea, but I hope no harm comes to children with this one."

Lindsey took the comm back as the queen hurried down and was lost in the crowd of excited females.

"Must be a very formal Earth custom for the queen to request it for her birthing day gift."

Lindsey took a deep breath and scanned the edge of the room where dozens of males stood looking fierce, intimidating, deadly... and confused as hell. "You heard the queen, gentlemen. Line up. Straight rows. Cover the dance floor. This is for the queen's birthday gift."

When the males grumbled and didn't move fast enough, Prime Nial moved to stand at the front of the room, Ander next to him. Ander's scowl was enough to encourage every slow foot.

"Fuck."

"Let's go, your lordship. Looks like even you aren't getting out of this." Sambor clipped me on the back, hard, and stepped forward to take his place in one of the lines. Full armor. Weapon. The works, since he was here as my personal guard and we'd both come directly from a day of meetings at IC Command. Next to him, a petite female in a sparkling gown and Atlan mating cuffs twirled and giggled in anticipation. On her other side, a freakishly monstrous cyborg with matching cuffs hovered protectively, clearly as confused as Sambor and I by the upcoming ritual.

By the gods, I hoped this line dance ceremony did not take too long. I had a warm bed waiting, since tomorrow would be another busy day at IC Command. Duty came first, as ambassador, in work and at events like these that were meant for pleasure. It was hard to relax after spending the day with Helion, the head of IC, and knowing another stressful day would follow in the morning. No doubt Sambor—and Lord Ander, who'd been part of the Prillon Prime contingency—agreed. But as the guest of honor's second mate, this held more satisfaction for Ander, meaning more disappointment at dawn when he would have to leave his mate's bed.

I stood next to Sambor and paid no attention to the bodies lining up next to us, behind us. The queen and her two mates were in the front row. If Prime Nial and Lord Ander were participating in this human ritual, there was no excuse not to.

Lindsey pointed to various females and warriors in the room to give instructions. *Move there. Stand here. You two, back one row.* It went on for about a minute until she was satisfied with the appearance and placement of everyone in the room.

"Good." She looked at the comm tech. "Let me get in line and then start. Okay?"

He nodded gravely, as if she'd given him a life-or-death order, then watched as she scrambled to stand next to the Elite Hunter she'd identified as hers a few moments ago.

Being a worthy male, he kissed her senseless before the music started.

I approved. If a male was going to claim a female for his own, he'd damn well better take excellent care of her. That included kissing her into dazed submission as often as possible.

The comm tech looked to Lindsey, who nodded. Then to the queen, who nodded as well. My entire being tensed in dread as he reached forward and activated the strange human music again. This was a different song. A stringed instrument filled the air with a pounding beat behind it as the females all clapped along.

"Perhaps this version has no voicing," Sambor mused.

We were not to be so lucky.

"Follow along, everyone. And one-two-three-four!" Lindsey shouted.

On the next beat, the ladies stepped forward. Then backward. The males scrambled to imitate the movements, but none of us had a clue what was happening next.

"This is strange, Nik. But at least they are all moving together now."

Sambor was right. The ladies moved as one, stomping, clapping. Running into the males.

Laughing.

The human voice spoke words that made no sense.

"*...tell my lips to tell my fingertips...*"

The whining male's voice seemed to repeat over and over in a strange cadence that was singularly annoying. "Why would a male speak to his own fingertips?" I asked. "Human males make no sense."

Sambor, who seemed to be learning the steps with an ease that made me want to trip him, grinned as he executed a perfect turn on his heel. "The male's heart is aching and breaking. However, the ladies seem to enjoy the idea of a male in pain."

As the song repeated a lyric about a male's heart blowing up inside his own body and killing him, the ladies stomped in unison, yelled out with excitement and clapped before starting the whole thing over again.

"Human females are, apparently, a bloodthirsty and merciless species when it comes to mating," I muttered.

Sambor nodded in agreement. "And I thought Prillon females were ruthless."

Two Atlan Warlords rammed into each other, one letting out a bellow of irritation seconds before his mate whirled into his arms and pulled him away. Then there was Commander and Lady Karter. She had the moves down, and beside her, Karter himself had picked it up. He was moving to the music and... fuck, he was enjoying himself. When he spun around in a circle, I saw the pleasure alighting his face.

Who would have guessed that Commander Karter could dance?

"To the right!" Lindsey shouted.

As one, the ladies turned to face the right, and Sambor and I hurried to keep pace. I was not going to humiliate myself by running into...

"Oh!"

Softness. A squeal. A small human female fell toward me after I'd run into her like a giant Atlan oaf.

"My lady! My apologies." I caught her in my arms, and she pressed into my chest, the dark green and gold gown she wore fluttering about my legs as the forward momentum of her fall had her softness, her feminine scent enveloping me completely.

I forgot to move with the group, staring down into a pair of bright green eyes. Her hair was a halo of auburn fire, and there was a small gold ring teasing me where it pierced the delicate flesh of her adorable little nose. I blinked, frozen as if stunned by an ion pistol.

Was she from Trion? The piercing made me wonder, but her gown was not typical of that planet's females. Nor did I feel piercings or a chain where the hard pebbles of her nipples pressed into my chest. Gods help me, she was beautiful, and my body responded with instant demand. My cock hardened, and my pulse pounded while I fought for control. Where was her mate? Her protector? I knew I should look around for a male who would be eager to take her from me, but I could not move.

She smiled up at me, her fair cheeks coloring under my attention to a perfect pink that matched her lips. Her full, open lips. I stood frozen, unable to look away.

"Sorry." Her breathless apology made my cock jump as the tremble in her voice was all I needed to imagine hearing that aching struggle for air under different circumstances... like when I filled her with my cock as Sambor held her in place for my claiming. When she was well pleasured, mindless with need, he would take her from behind as I held her body locked to mine, as we made her ours.

Fuck. I was insane. Right now there was most likely a pair of Prillon warriors or an Atlan Warlord preparing to remove my head from my body for holding her like this.

Close. Feet off the floor. In my arms and under my protection as if she were mine.

Sambor rammed into us from the side.

I threw an elbow to protect the small female in my arms from the armored giant, and he flew backward, landing with a thud against the Atlan who lifted *his* mate out of the way with a speed I'd learned to appreciate on the battlefield.

The Atlan bellowed a warning. Sambor landed in a crouched position, snarling back.

"Rezzer, I'm fine." The female reached up and placed her palm on the Warlord's cheek. Instantly he calmed. She turned her gaze to me and then the female I held. Her eyes widened; then she grinned, a wicked sort of silent communication moving between the two human females. "Vegas?"

The woman in my arms glanced at me, then at the woman. "Maybe!"

I had no idea what that meant. "My name is not Vegas, my lady," I told her.

Rezzer looked to me, to my arms where they remained wrapped around the female. "Lucy, has this male harmed you?"

"Of course not," she replied, her voice melodic and filled with happiness. Her name was *Lucy*.

The huge Atlan crossed his arms and stared me down. This imposing action caused Sambor to stand quickly and move in close to my side, just in case the beast decided we'd harmed his mate or challenged him.

"Really, Rezz, I'm fine. I promise," Lucy added. "I tripped and he caught me. That's all."

The Atlan tilted his head as if deciding whether or not to believe the female. His gaze narrowed. "Then why are his arms still about you?"

A Hunter bumped into the back of the Atlan, which did nothing more than make him frown. Huge fucker. And with the Hive tech implants I'd caught glimpses of, he was probably even more dangerous than the average Atlan, which was downright savage.

"Because you aliens can't dance to save your lives. That one tripped and was about to run me over," Lucy countered, pointing at Sambor, who actually turned from his usual golden tone to a much darker brown, closer to my coloring than I'd ever seen him, even in the heat of battle.

My second was *embarrassed*.

I wasn't sure if I was *saving her life*, but I'd go with that if it kept her in my arms. "I would never harm a female."

The Warlord grunted in agreement, and his stance relaxed. "I gave my word to Warlord Wulf to protect her while he is on Earth with his mate." His neutral face gave way to a frown. "I knew bringing an unmated female to this planet would be a mistake."

I heard one word... *unmated*. Setting the female gently on her feet, I kept my arm around her as I bowed low to the Warlord whose next words might very well determine my fate. "I am Lord Niklas Lorvar of Prillon Prime. Cousin to Battlegroup Commander Lorvar. Ambassador and trusted advisor of Prime Nial." Warlord Wulf was this female's protector? How had that happened? "And this is Captain Sambor Treval, close cousin to Hunt Treval of The Colony."

"You are Hunt's cousin?" He looked to Sambor, who nodded gravely.

"Hunt and I grew up together. He will confirm this. I am a warrior of honor. I would never harm a female," Sambor assured him.

The Atlan paused as if considering. Around the room, several more Atlans and more than one Prillon duo had begun to take an interest in our conversation as well.

Fuck. Attention was not what I wanted, not with this beautiful female in my arms.

"I assure you, Warlord, I am a male of honor. Lucy is safe with me," I tried to ease the overly protective beast and nearly held my breath as I waited for his decision. Would he leave Lucy in my care? Or steal her from my arms before I had a chance to learn what might please her? Make her sigh? Moan? Scream in pleasure?

"Leave Lucy be," the Atlan's mate said to him. "These guys will *take care* of her."

I didn't miss the way she grinned when she said that, although I wasn't exactly sure why.

"Come on, Rezzer. Dance with me," she continued, tugging on his uniform shirt. "I'll show you the moves."

With one last glance at me accompanied by a snarl of warning—as if I didn't know that to harm a single hair on Lucy's head would mean my death—he allowed his mate to lead him back into the steps of the strange dance.

Lucy melted against my side once the Warlord moved on.

"That was intense," she said, then looked up into my eyes, and I forgot we were standing in the middle of a roomful of people. "Thanks for catching me."

"My pleasure." The words were idiotic, but I didn't care. Touching her was a pleasure. As was looking into her gaze, tracing the outline of her lips with my fingertip.

"Really, Niklas?" Sambor asked, jostling me enough to break the hypnotic hold the female seemed to have on me. I looked up to find him grinning. "Starting fights? I thought you were a diplomat."

"I believe it was you who said something about

enjoying ourselves." My gaze locked with Sambor's, and I tipped my head down to indicate the human in my arms. This female was beautiful. Stunning. My cock remained hard despite every attempt my mind made to reason with the insolent organ.

She was here as a friend of the queen. She was human. How was it possible she did not have a mate?

Or two?

Or three? Surely she belonged to someone.

I'd seen more than one group of Viken fighters escorting a female tonight, including the queen and kings of Viken carrying their two precious daughters. Both with dark red hair like their mother.

Like Lucy.

"Holy fuck," Sambor murmured just above a whisper when he got a good look at the female in my arms. He went rigid, and when one of the kings of Viken stepped on his foot and offered apologies, he didn't even blink.

I looked down and drowned in her gaze, my entire body going as rigid as my cock. She wasn't squirming or fighting to be somewhere else. It seemed she liked being held as much as I liked holding her.

"Are you not frightened?" I asked, my voice loud enough to be heard over the music.

"Of you or your terrible dancing?" She actually laughed, setting the fiery curls around her face to bouncing. The rest she had twisted up on top of her head in some strange configuration common among females. "Either way, the answer is no. You're actually kind of smaller than I'm used to."

I wasn't sure if I should laugh at her boldness or feel insulted. I was nearly seven feet tall, by no means *small*.

"Only Atlans are larger than Prillons. You are mated to a beast then?" Sambor asked. Had he not heard the Atlan, Rezzer, grumble about her being unmated? Or was he simply seeking confirmation? Our gazes dropped to inspect her wrists, which were bare. No mating cuffs.

When the Viken king bumped into Sambor again, I'd had enough. I picked her up and walked out of the dancing throng. Lucy did not resist. But when we reached the side of the room, I had no choice but to set her back upon her feet.

Her smile was open, welcoming and curious as she glanced up at the two of us. "To answer your question, no. I don't have a mate."

"Based on the ring in your nose, I assumed a mate from Trion," I said, looking again for the outline of similar adornments in her nipples.

"Nope, no Trion mate, nor am I seeking one. From any planet."

"You're not? I understand that human females were only allowed to leave your planet to mate or fight in the war," Sambor said to her. Earth was one of only a handful of all planets that allowed their females to fight, a decision both Sambor and I disagreed with, not because a female couldn't hold her own in battle, but because we were more than willing to sacrifice our own lives so they did not have to.

Apparently Lucy did not approve of Sambor's words. She frowned and I did not like to see the crease mar her smooth brow. "Wow. Know everything about us, do you? I understood that a Prillon male got tested for a bride because he couldn't find one on his own."

I couldn't help the smile at the way Sambor's eyes widened at her well-countered words or the way he bowed his head slightly.

"My apologies. Lucy, correct?" he asked.

"Yes."

"Then if you are not here to acquire a mate, why are you here?"

Her bright green eyes glanced between me and Sambor with... unhidden desire. Lust. Open and blatant appreciation.

Need.

My cock punched against my pants, eager to get to her, to fulfill any need she might have. I envisioned her in bed between Sambor and me. Naked. Our hands and mouths on her. Our cocks in her. I could almost hear her moans of pleasure, screams of satisfaction.

She set her hand on my chest, and I felt the heat of it through my tunic. Fuck, she was a contrary thing. Tiny and frail, yet a tongue sharper than a Viken's most ruthless blade. Lightness and now this... heat.

Taking a step closer, she placed her palm in the same spot on Sambor. "I am here to enjoy myself. To have some fun."

"Please do not let us stop you from dancing some more." I would deny her nothing, and I had to admit watching her dance would be quite erotic. "Unless the queen bids otherwise, we will remain here and watch."

"I want you to do more than watch me." Or at least that's what I thought she said—her voice had dipped almost to a whisper. "So you're a lord?" she asked, louder this time, her thumb sliding back and forth across my chest, distracting me.

I imagined that thumb sliding over the crown of my cock, and I was ready to toss her over my shoulder and carry her off to an empty room in the palace so she could do so.

Her scent filled my head, and my heart raced as if I'd just outrun a Hive scout in a stealth fighter. "My *name* is Niklas."

"Nik."

I'd never heard anyone shorten my name before, but the abbreviation made me want to yell *mine* so everyone could hear me over the thrum of loud music. Gods, she was a bold little thing. No Prillon female would make such forward contact with a male. She licked her lips in Sambor's direction.

"And you?" She looked up at Sambor, who was armed and had to be almost two heads taller than the petite female, yet she appeared unafraid.

"I am Sambor Treval." He set his hand over hers and bowed slightly at the waist.

"Sam and Nik." She sighed like we'd revealed the secrets of the universe and filled her with bliss. I suddenly wanted to hear more sounds from her small throat. I wanted to hear her beg, hear the soft cries of her release. Sighs of surrender. I imagined stripping the wispy green fabric from her body, unwinding the golden strands that crisscrossed her waist and breasts as if unwrapping a gift.

"Are you two together?" Her green gaze flitted

between the two of us. "You know, like a warrior and his second?"

Fuck. My cock jerked to attention as Sambor nodded. "Yes, I am his chosen second."

"How can we assist you, my lady? A beverage?" I asked, trying to regain control of my body after the gut punch that was this small, human female. Bouncing red curls, pale skin too even and perfect to be real. Her green eyes were lined with dark accents that made them appear larger, more innocent. Obviously the work of magic as she was not acting as an innocent would.

She was pure seduction. Beauty.

"Orgasms."

I coughed, stunned by her boldness. Sambor laughed.

"Orgasms?" Sambor repeated.

"I've spent too many nights alone in my bed." She looked us up and down; then her gaze remained on *down,* on our cocks. Mine was rock-hard and pressing against my pants. I had no doubt Sambor suffered a similar affliction. "I was hoping that maybe, while I'm here, you two might want to join me?" Her words were bold, but her gaze was averted, unsure—now that she'd offered herself to us.

Yet there was no denying her sincerity. Or her need. I inhaled deeply, scented her feminine heat, the sweet perfume of her skin. Her pussy, hot and wet and eager. For me and Sambor. Together.

"You want us to see to your pleasure," Sambor said. Everyone but the guards were dancing. Still, he kept his voice low. "Touch you. Fuck you. Make you scream your release?"

Leave it to Sambor to be crude, but her eyelids flared in shock, then dropped to hide her desire. Her pink tongue flicked out to wet her lower lip. "Yes. That's what I want."

I lifted my palm to cup the side of her face and gently angled it toward mine, waited with what felt like infinite patience for her to open her eyes. When she did, I nearly groaned. Her green gaze was flooded with honesty. Need. Trust.

Submission.

Unable to resist, I ran my thumb along her plump lower lip, imagined it wrapped around my cock.

She offered herself. The raw hunger that slammed through my body made my decision a simple one. I chose to accept. The party continued all around us. It seemed Sambor and I would have a party of our own. A smaller, more intimate one with just one guest. Who needed to sample the Earth cake that was on display when we could eat Lucy from Earth?

3

I TRIED TO REMAIN CALM. To keep my gaze on theirs as I waited for their answer to my question. If they rejected me, I'd die. Okay, not really, but a little bit inside. Living on The Colony with several other women from Earth and watching them all hot and heavy with their mates was hard enough. Especially seeing my BFF Olivia with Wulf.

I thought for sure I'd have a mate of my own by now. 'd been spending too much time with my vibrator and none with a real, live, flesh-and-blood male. If I bombed at propositioning two Prillons into a one-night stand, then I was going to be devastated. That vibrator I was tired of would need an upgrade because my lady parts were only going to see mechanical devices from now on.

This was the trip to go wild. Sure, the palace of Prillon

Prime was a far cry from Las Vegas, but it was the time for me to get drunk, flash my boobs and wake up with a sore pussy and the inability to walk properly.

These two Prillons were gorgeous. Seriously out-of-this-world hot.

Sambor was like a golden god, every inch of him gleaming like he'd been touched by King Midas. Golden skin and hair, a darker gold in his eyes. His angular Prillon features made him striking, like a perfect beach model someone would use for a cologne ad. A sun god.

Then there was Nik. Hair so dark it was nearly black, his eyes a startling and very alien bright copper, and his dark, smooth skin reminded me of melted milk chocolate chips when they were warm from the oven. I would take a golden cookie and tear it in half and lift the dark, dripping chocolate onto my tongue.

What did a Prillon's cum taste like? Was it salty? Sweet? Did Nik's skin taste like chocolate? Did Sambor's golden skin taste like metal? Like vanilla? Like sunshine? I was an artist at heart, and color palettes were my life. I had dozens of names floating in my head, ideas to describe these two males and their unique coloring. I wanted to see more. No. I wanted to see *everything*.

I wanted to touch. And taste. What did their kiss taste like? Their skin? Did they growl or bellow or moan when they came? What did their cocks look like? How *human* was the rest of them?

Were they having similar thoughts? Because they continued to stare and stare, as if I'd said I was actually a Hive Scout.

Okay, I had my answer. Or a nonanswer. My anticipation drained out of me like I was a helium balloon and they'd just stabbed me with a knife. Yeah, it was time to go before I wilted completely and sank to the ground in a puddle of embarrassment. Time to go strip off this gorgeous gown and put on my usual sweats and transport back to The Colony.

I tried to pull my hands away from their muscled chests, but neither allowed it. They held on tight.

"I do not have a problem with giving you pleasure," Nik said. "Do you, Sambor?"

"Absolutely not."

Relief coursed through me and I sighed. I couldn't help the smile. "Good." I glanced over my shoulder at everyone dancing. "Now would be the time to duck out. Rezzer's not the only one keeping an eye on me."

Nik's eyes lifted and looked out over my head at the guests, scanning.

"I am pleased to hear you are protected; however, you have nothing to fear from us," Nik vowed.

They might stand like two huge giants, but I was used to Wulf's hulking size and I wasn't scared of him. Sure, Wulf might bluster and be a pain in my ass, but he'd never hurt me. Same for Braun, who was huge, cyborg, and, I suspected, fighting a serious case of Atlan mating fever. Not that he'd said as much. Braun would not pressure a female that way. In fact, not one alien I'd met would ever harm a female. As for these two Prillons, I wasn't afraid of either of them. I was nervous as hell. Horny, definitely. I had never, *ever* propositioned a guy before. I wasn't a virgin, but I'd never gone up to a stranger—*two* strangers—and said I wanted orgasms.

These weren't boring, tame Earth guys either. They were Prillons. Bossy, protective and dominant. They ran battle-groups without breaking a sweat.

I wasn't sure if I was crazy good or crazy bad. When I looked them over again, I was definitely crazy *bad*. I waggled my finger at the front of their pants. "Except for those. My pussy is a little afraid of what's in there. Got ion pistols in your pocket or are you very pleased with my offer?"

They frowned in tandem. Yeah, I used sarcasm as a defense mechanism when I was nervous. It seemed, though, that I confused these guys. I laughed. "Do I make your cocks hard?"

I watched Nik swallow hard. "Fuck, yes."

I licked my lips and said, "Then we should go to my room."

"Fuck, yes," Sam echoed.

This time, when I tried to move my hands from their chests, they let me. I wrapped my fingers around theirs and led them from the room, the music and everyone else at the party fading away. The country music anthem we'd all been line dancing to faded into the song from *Pretty in Pink*'s prom scene. I wasn't going to be missed. And if I was, all the girls would think I'd found my Las Vegas–style fling.

I might be a little bit crazy for leading two huge aliens to my room, but I wasn't stupid. I'd stay at the palace with guards around. All I had to do was scream and I'd have an entourage of royal guards swarming.

The farther we got from the public area of the palace and closer to the guest wing, all that was left was me and two Prillon hunks... and their huge, hard cocks. By the time I closed the door to the beautiful bedroom I'd been given, I'd lost some of my boldness. My brain was trying to slut shame me into changing my mind, but my body was ready. My panties were ruined. My nipples were hard.

I'd planned this. A weekend away, although there was no such thing as a *weekend* in space. Wulf wasn't in the room to rip Sam's and Nik's heads off to protect my honor. He wasn't even on the planet. Or in the same part of the galaxy. He was on Earth with Olivia, doing talk shows. Ha!

This was my time.

I had two guys with eager brains *and* cocks as they eyed me.

Waiting.

The energy between us practically crackled, the intensity of their gazes, their need almost tangible.

For me.

That controlled power had me almost whimpering, but I bit my lip to hold it back. I wanted to feel it when they touched me. Kissed me. Fucked me.

A throaty sound escaped.

Nik's eyes flared. Sam's narrowed.

They breathed hard. Deep, as if they could scent me, knew that I was wet for them.

That gave me the boldness I needed to continue.

I took Nik's hand, and I gasped again. His skin was hot to the touch, as if he were an inferno and I was going to get burned. I felt the calluses on his palm, a sign he worked hard with his body. These two weren't just posh dignitaries who'd come to their queen's party. Sam was clearly a fighter. A guy in a uniform was hot even in space. As for Nik, I didn't know what he did, but his muscled physique filled out his Prillon dress clothes in ways a political blowhard from Earth never could. Hell, not one of the males at the party were built anything but huge, fit and hunky.

Nik followed silently over to a plush chair in front of the window. With a hand on his chest, I gave him a push, and he dropped into the seat. He was doing exactly as I wanted, as if I were the aggressor here. If he hadn't wanted to sit, my little nudge would have had no effect. His hands rested on the arms of the chair, seemingly relaxed. His neck was taut, and I felt his energy, the tension in him, all directed at me.

I glanced over my shoulder at Sam.

Why weren't they pouncing? Why weren't they pushing me up against a wall? Bending me over a flat surface? Pressing me into a soft bed? "I thought Prillons were all alpha and bossy," I said.

Sam approached. For such a huge guy, he was practically silent as he settled beside me, arms crossed over his chest. "Do I not look alpha and bossy?"

I laughed. "You look like you just came from battle."

He cocked his head to the side, studying me. "Battle, no. Niklas and I only returned from our day's mission a short time before the party."

I glanced at the ion pistol strapped to the holster on his thigh. Then the tree-trunk thigh. Then the rest of him in black and with armor, all badass. "Yes, you look very alpha and bossy."

Sam nodded toward Nik. "As for him, he might not wear armor, but Niklas is an ambassador. This week alone he's worked with the head of IC to interrogate a Hive Nexus unit, tracked down criminals on Rogue 5 and managed to show up for the queen's surprise birthing day celebration freshly bathed."

I'd heard of the IC. Jessica had told me it was like the CIA, only with more power and they had to deal with the Hive as well as all the usual—spies, weapons dealers, drug dealers, slave traders. All of it sounded pretty bad. The fact that Nik had to work with the head of that branch of the Coalition told me a lot about his status and level of responsibility. Although I had no idea exactly what an *ambassador* did out in space. Didn't sound like he shook hands and kissed babies. Not by the rippling muscles and calloused hands or the mention of a captured Hive prisoner.

Nik stayed silent as I stared at him, although he did arch a dark eyebrow. The contrast between them was making me swoon. They didn't look human—their features were too angular, Sam's gold skin and Nik's copper-colored eyes not like *anything* I would have seen on Earth. But God, they were big, muscled bad boys if I'd ever seen one. And I *wanted.*

Swallowing hard, I compared myself to them. I was average height and a bit too curvy to be fashionable back home. My hair wasn't just red, it was a dark, curly auburn that I'd been told matched my temper. I was pasty white with my makeup on and burned if I didn't slather on sunscreen. No one knew what I really looked like under my armor.

Well, no one but Olivia, and she wasn't here.

I was covered in freckles, especially my face, arms and shoulders. The redhead's curse. I looked like a speckled freak without the magic of liquid and powders I spread across my skin before I set foot out of my bedroom.

Covered.

I wasn't smooth-skinned and stunning like the other ladies. Queen Jessica was the perfect, *Barbie* blonde. Rachel had that dark hair and skin the color of a perfect latte going on. Lindsey, Kristin and Caroline were fair, like me, but they weren't cursed with a road map of spots covering every inch of their bodies. I shouldn't even get started about Mikki, with her perfectly straight black hair and petite, athletic surfer's body. She didn't have a speck of cellulite.

"That's... impressive." I ran my hand over my hair, which had been pulled back into a pretty twist I'd thought would show off my bare shoulders.

No, not bare. Covered in makeup. And the twist had been just as much about hiding the wild curls as about the overall look. Not that my plan had worked. My hair had a mind of its own, and my face was framed with escapees.

Who was I kidding right now? I wasn't ready to reveal myself to these two godlike warriors.

I was not what these aliens expected from a human female. I didn't look like any of the others, nor surely any females they might have met in the Coalition. If the freckles weren't enough, the red curls pushed me over the edge from cute to... odd. Even the queen of Viken had straight, perfect red hair and unmarked skin. I looked like a road map without the roads connecting the dots.

Maybe this wasn't a good idea after all.

Or maybe I could do this and not get naked? Would they do me in my dress?

Nik held out his hand, and I realized I'd been standing like a mute, staring at him for far too long. Not wanting to give myself time to panic, I stepped closer and placed my hand in his. His huge, warm fingers wrapped around mine, and something inside me settled instantly. Like he'd just unplugged the panic button and set me on a slow, warm simmer.

I could do this. If they didn't like me, I never had to see them again. One and done.

"We do not have the advantage of a mating collar surrounding your neck, Lady Lucy," Nik said, his voice calm and even. Yeah, I doubted he was having body image issues right about now. I doubted either guy was modest. "We do not know what you are feeling. You will have to tell us."

Oh shit. "Mating collar?" I squeaked, then swallowed hard. "I don't want a mating collar." Just to make that perfectly clear. This was a one-night stand. Mikki, Kristin and Rachel all had a collar, and I knew what it meant, the *power* of it. "I have to return to The Colony after the birthday ball. I'm only here for two more days. Two days."

"You must return there for your work?" Niklas asked.

I put my hand to my chest. "Me? No. On Earth I cut and styled women's hair. Well, some guys, too. I worked with Olivia on the *Bachelor Beast* show doing makeup. I'm a makeup artist and hairstylist."

Sam's pale brows winged up. "I've heard of the Earth comm program. It is fortunate I am not an Atlan, as that did not sound enjoyable for Warlord Wulf."

I shrugged. "He found his mate, so he thinks it was worth it."

Both of them looked me over. "Yes, I can understand," Nik said, glancing at my hair. "Did you style yourself tonight?"

I patted my curls. "Yes."

"The color is lovely. Everything about you is beautiful. Is styling females necessary on The Colony?"

I held up my hand to stop his words. "Necessary? No. Not on The Colony. There are only a few women. Besides, my goal is bigger than just being a stylist."

"Oh?" Sam asked. "What is your desire?"

"To run a spa. A place for women—females—to go to relax, to pamper their bodies and make themselves feel confident and beautiful. I want to give them a place to take care of themselves."

"That is a mate's job," Nik added.

"No. It's really not. If a woman feels good about herself, then that comes out in everything she does. I want to help with that."

"You wish to care for others' health and well-being. Your goal is admirable."

I gave Niklas a funny look. "Admirable? I'm talking about makeovers and massages. What you guys do is admirable."

Sam stepped up behind me, his hands gentle as he placed them on my shoulders. I could feel the heat radiating from him. "If not for this work, then why must you return to The Colony so soon?"

"My family is there. I will not abandon them."

"Family? I thought you were unmated."

"I consider my best friend, Olivia, and her mate, Wulf, my family. They have two small children with them, Olivia's niece and nephew. Long story. They're not blood, but they're mine nonetheless."

That was as clear as I could make it. Olivia, Tanner and Emma—and now Wulf, too, the big, overprotective lug—were mine. I loved them with every cell in my body. *Aunt Woocy* would never abandon them.

Sambor's lips settled against the curve of my neck where it met my shoulders, and I was once more pleased with my decision to put my hair up and out of the way as a shiver raced through me. I was sure he could see and feel the goose bumps on my skin.

"Two days then. So, my lady, along with orgasms, exactly what do you want with us?" Niklas asked, his gaze locked on mine as Sam's lips lingered and desire rocketed through me. "Have you been with two males before?"

"No."

"Are you a virgin, Lucy?" Sam whispered, his breath fanning my ear. His hands didn't move from where they rested atop the curves of my hips, and the heat seemed to be amplified by the fact that Nik watched. These were warriors, not schoolboys. They were aliens. Protective. Obsessive. I'd seen how Maxim and Ryston were with Rachel. Hunt and Tyran with Kristin. I knew this could go sideways if I wasn't careful.

"No. I'm not a virgin. I want sex. Hot sex. And yes,

orgasms. Ones I don't have to give myself. Then I want to go home."

Sam chuckled and the sound felt like it vibrated through my skull. "You want to use us for your pleasure and walk away?"

Well, when he put it that way, I sounded like a total piece-of-shit human being. But yes, that was exactly what I wanted. "On Earth, we call it a one-night stand." I cleared my throat, more nervous than I wanted to think about. "I guess, technically, I want two nights—and a date to the royal ball. But then I'm going home."

Sam wrapped his arms around my waist from behind, his chin now resting on my shoulder as he looked at Nik. "I have no problem with that. Niklas?"

Nik looked from Sam to me, and his gaze locked with mine as the heat of Sam's entire body melted me from behind. His hard cock pressed to my back, and I held off a groan by sheer force of will. I *wanted* this. Them. The males on The Colony were sexy, amazing warriors, but none had managed to make me *feel* as much as Nik and Sam had in the last few minutes.

I was in trouble here. I knew it. I just wasn't sure how much. I'd been bold and brave and propositioned them and taken them to my room. I did *not* want to walk away. I *wanted* to get naked, touch them everywhere, taste them. Sleep between them and know I was totally and completely protected. Safe. Wanted. I needed to feel beautiful and desired and like a woman instead of a nanny. At least for a couple of days. I didn't want to go to one more stupid event as Olivia's and Wulf's third wheel. I needed a break from taking care of everyone else.

Making others look pretty. For once I wanted to do something for myself.

"Niklas?" Sam lifted his head and removed his hands. Suddenly the room chilled, and I shuddered at the loss of his heat. The green and gold dress I wore was fairy-tale princess gorgeous, but it wasn't thick. In fact, the soft material clung to every curve but didn't do much to hold in the heat.

Nik didn't look at Sam. He still watched me. "We are males of worth. Of honor. Based on your words, you are not ours to claim. If you want as you described, my lady, we are at your service. You must take what you need."

"Thank the gods." Sam's statement was followed by the sounds of him eagerly removing his boots. Armor hit the floor next.

All while Nik's gaze locked with mine. There was a challenge in his eyes. A dare. He waited for me to do just as he'd said. I had to *take what I needed.* I was in charge.

I licked my lips, lifted my chin and said, "Take off your clothes, Lord Niklas. I want to look at you."

Slowly he stood to remove his dark blue tunic. My mouth practically watered as he revealed sculpted abs and a massive chest. Definitely not a desk jockey.

Heart pounding, I looked over my shoulder at a nearly naked Sam. He'd left some sort of soft underpants on, something that must have been beneath his armor. His golden body was even more massive, more muscled —like that was possible. And his cock? It strained against the black fabric like a wild thing aching to break free.

"You too, Sam. Stand over there." I pointed to the spot next to Nik. "I want to see both of you."

Sam looked at Nik for permission to move, which both fascinated and annoyed me. I narrowed my gaze at Nik, feeling my feminine power now. "I told him to move. He might be your second, but I thought I was in charge here."

Nik's gaze darkened even further, the copper turning a burnt color I'd never seen before, but it made my pussy clench with heat. Teasing him, taunting the beast was *fun.*

It seemed he liked it, too.

"I will allow you to set the pace, my lady, to take what you need from us, but you were never in charge."

Shit, that was true. They could dominate me. Good and bad. They weren't because it was Nik's choice to *allow* me to guide them. To take what I wanted.

"I allow you to set the pace, but your pleasure is mine."

Double shit. I'd said I wanted orgasms from them. I was at their mercy, no matter how bossy I was.

Fine. I had some ways to make his control crumble. I reached for the ties that loosened my dress. Pulled them. Held my arms over my head like a goddess as the fabric slid silently down my body to pool at my feet. Beneath, I wore a strapless lace push-up bra and G-string panties. Green, to match my dress. And my eyes.

The Coalition's S-Gen machine came in handy after one learned to use it properly.

Neither male moved as they took in the human underwear. They both looked—dumbstruck.

I smiled. God, did this feel good. They hadn't said a word about the freckles that covered my legs and back.

And unlike some of the other ladies, I had decided to keep a nice little landing strip *down there.*

They hadn't seen that. Yet. They stood side by side, shirtless. Hard cocks straining against the fabric. That kind of reaction couldn't be faked, and the dark spots of pre-cum wetting their clothes made me feel even more powerful. They were mine right now. To do with as I pleased. The high-and-mighty lord of Prillon Prime had spoken, and I believed him.

Mine. Mine. Mine. Both of them.

"Shall I continue, Lord Niklas? Sambor?"

"Yes." They answered as one and I smiled.

"Get naked."

They immediately did as I asked, and my knees wobbled when I saw what they'd been hiding. Two cocks. One golden. One a deep, luscious brown. Both big. Hard. Eager.

They stood before me bare. Cocks long and thick and pointed right at me.

Placing my hand on Nik's chest, I pushed him back down into the chair. Again he allowed it. "I want you," I said, although that was pretty much a given.

His silence was all the encouragement I needed to keep going. I set one knee beside his hip, then the other, straddling him. I crawled up his body, kissing and licking as I went. He shuddered, but his hands remained rigid on the arms of the chair. Sam watched; the sound of his ragged breathing had me reaching out to wrap one hand around his cock as I claimed Nik's lips in a kiss.

I tasted him. Explored. For all of five seconds.

Then Nik's hand was in my hair, his mouth taking

mine with a ruthless desire I had no hope of resisting. He plundered my mouth as I squeezed and rubbed Sam's cock, mimicking the movements of my tongue as I dueled with Nik.

Nik pulled my hair, and I moaned at the slight sting of pain. It had me rubbing my body against his hard cock. Reaching up, I released the front hook of my bra and threw the damn thing across the room. I wanted skin on skin. I wanted Nik's hard cock inside me. I wanted Sam clawing for sanity as I worked him with my tongue. I wanted to *conquer* them both like a badass bedroom warrior. I might leave in two days, but I wanted them to think of me every single time they touched a woman for the rest of their lives. I wanted to be *that girl.* The one that haunted them. The one they could never forget. The wild, uninhibited bad girl that I so totally was *not.*

"Rip the panties off," I ordered, my breath ragged.

Nik looked at me as if he didn't want to obey. But I wasn't having it. "Rip them off. I can make more." I lifted my hips, rubbing the wet scrap of fabric that covered my clit and pussy over the hard length of him.

That was all it took. With a growl and a sharp snap, they were gone. But I still wasn't exactly where I wanted to be.

Slowly, deliberately, I removed Nik's hand from my hair and placed it back on the chair. His other hand had not left my ass once my undies were gone, so I wrapped my fingers around his and moved that hand to the chair as well.

His chest heaved, but he watched me. Waiting.

Looking up at Sam, I removed my hand from his body

and rose onto my knees. Glancing from one to the other, I had to make sure they were going to let me do this. I was getting consent from them. "Anything I want?"

"Anything, my lady," Sam agreed. This time his voice was deeper. Raspy.

"Yes." Nik's one-word response was so restrained I wondered if he was going to bust a blood vessel in his head.

I moved then, standing long enough to turn around. I reached for Sam and pulled his head toward me, kissed him the way I'd kissed Nik. All heat and tongue and lust as I melted into his arms. He wrapped me up, the long stretch of his chest hot and hard against me.

"Enough." I ignored Nik's command; however, Sambor obeyed at once, setting me back on my feet. His chest heaved, and I knew he was mine now, just like his impatient friend behind me.

With a grin up at Sam, I backed up to settle once more into Nik's lap, but now I faced away from him. Reaching behind me, I placed the head of his cock at the entrance of my wet, aching core. I slid onto him slowly, confident the medical team I'd visited on The Colony had taken care of any pregnancy or other concerns. No condom was needed in space. I was free to... enjoy. God, just the way he stretched me open, the way he filled me so completely, I was going to do just that.

I wiggled, using my legs to rise and fall on his hard length, taking a bit more of him every time. He groaned, his hands in fists on the arms of the chair, exactly where I had placed them.

Finally he was all the way in, and I sat once again upon his sturdy thighs. I'd taken every long inch of him.

I curled my finger. "Sam, come here." My words were urgent, breathy, and I was relieved when he came to stand before me. Close enough so I could reach out and wrap both hands around his cock, one at the base and one at the tip as I shifted my hips and heard Nik moan behind me. "This cock is mine now, Sam."

I glanced up at him through my lashes. He looked stunned at my words, but I was beyond caring. I was going to make him lose his damn mind while I rode Nik's cock. I was going to make them both want more. And more. And more. I had two days. I wanted to spend every moment I could in bed with them. I had a lot of loving to cram into a short time, and I had found the perfect males.

Not one but two aliens to satisfy me.

Sam stepped closer, close enough that I could sit up straight and take him fully into my mouth, setting my hands on his thighs.

With one more glance up, I swallowed him down. Sucked. Licked. Didn't stop until I felt his balls swell up and his cock tighten just that little bit.

I stopped. Moved on Nik. Rolled my hips as I lifted and lowered, fucked myself on him in a random way that made my clit pulse, made my pussy clench. Reaching down between both of their legs, I cupped, then stroked their balls.

"By the gods, female." Sam threw his head back but didn't move, didn't make one demand.

Giving them a break, I lifted both of Nik's hands from

the arms of the chair and placed them over my breasts. "Touch me."

He needed no further encouragement, quickly sliding his thumbs back and forth over my hard nipples. Squeezed. Tugged. Learned what I liked. What made me gasp. And moan.

I took Sam back into my mouth as Nik's hand dropped between my widespread thighs to cover my clit. Tease. Stroke me as I moved over him.

It was too good. Too much. The feel of both men surrounding me. The sounds of fucking. The scent of it. The feel of them both so deep. I couldn't hold back. I wasn't going to try.

My body went off like a firecracker, and the spasms took over as both of my lovers sank into my body. As far as I could get them. I wanted them *inside me.* Completely. Where I was beginning to realize I might never get them out.

Nik moved beneath me, thrusting up into my tight pussy, my legs forced wider as he shifted forward and moved his knees apart.

I was open and vulnerable, his heat at my back, Sam's in front of me. I was between them, Nik's cock in my pussy, Sam in my mouth. Nik sat up, and his chest pressed to my back like an iron wall as his hands worked my body, one on my clit, the other up to rest wrapped around my throat. There was no pressure, but the touch made my pussy clench like a vise and he noticed my reaction. My pervy, orgasm-inducing reaction.

I *liked* feeling vulnerable. Open. Exposed. Knowing that he truly was in control.

Sam took his cue, and his hands fisted in my hair, pulling just hard enough to make me gasp. I couldn't move, couldn't get away from them as they both fucked me harder. Faster.

I screamed around Sam's cock when I came again, both of them following me over. Their hot cum felt like an anointment into another world. An alien world.

A fucking amazing universe of pleasure and heat and lust.

I had vainly wanted this night to haunt both of them, but I realized, as Nik stroked me to a third orgasm, his still-hard cock stretching me wide, Sam's taste on my tongue, that the joke was on me.

The only person who wasn't going to be able to forget tonight was me. When Sam reached down and lifted me off Nik's spent cock and carried me to bed, I knew we'd only gotten started.

4

*S*ambor, Transport Station 345, Prillon Prime

"I DON'T LIKE LEAVING HER," I grumbled. Again. "Especially after last night."

I leaned against the wall, arms crossed, the room crowded with a fighter squad armed and ready to transport to a battlegroup. Others, like us, waited to transport to their latest mission or destination. While I was back in my armor, prepared for battle, I wasn't going off to fight the Hive. I followed Niklas, and today we were to accompany Prime Nial's second, Lord Ander, to another security briefing hosted by one of my least favorite Prillon Warriors, Dr. Helion.

Niklas wore his usual ambassador attire. It wasn't an official uniform, especially not one of the Coalition, but his black pants and navy tunic indicated he was a high-level Prillon. A planetary representative. His role wasn't part of combat operations. He didn't personally battle the Hive, but he did direct the flow of weapons and fighters from other worlds, deal with interplanetary disputes, and act as Prime Nial's eyes and ears out in the political nightmare that helped hold the entire Interstellar Coalition of Planets together. Lots of egos. Lots of kings and queens, lords and ladies, commanders and captains, merchants and smugglers. Everyone had a role to play. And everyone had a price.

I thought his a terrible duty. My role was much simpler. I only had to protect him, kill if necessary. I didn't have to negotiate with the enemy. I didn't have to make them happy. Niklas was the smiling face Prime Nial presented to planetary leaders. And on Niklas's—or Prime Nial's—orders, I was the knife at their throat.

"I don't like it either," Niklas countered in a far from diplomatic tone.

The hum of the transport pad followed with a crackle of static as another transport was completed.

Of course, our balls had been emptied and our needs slaked multiple times over multiple hours. We should be relaxed and smiling. We *should* be anticipating our return from IC Command later this evening when we would see Lucy again. Touch her. Make her writhe and beg and scream her pleasure.

Instead we had to leave a naked, sleeping female in the warm bed we'd shared with no collar about her neck announcing our claim.

"Duty calls and not even a willing female can keep us from it," he added, watching a group of palace officials climb the steps to leave next.

"You focus too much on your role as ambassador. Even the Prime takes time from his duties to tend to other things, like his mate."

"I have had no reason to focus on anything else. While I'm not keen about Helion, he is dedicated, as I am."

I stared at him wide-eyed. "You wish to compare yourself to that asshole? I think he sleeps in the command room."

No one I'd met liked the head of IC. He was, as I'd said, an asshole.

"I did not sleep in the command room last night." Apparently Niklas felt the need to remind me of where we'd spent the last few hours. Not that I could forget. I could still taste Lucy on my tongue, scent her on my skin.

I thought of the sated, naked female and the warm bed we'd left to stand here and bicker. "Only because she propositioned you. Us." I paused, worried. "Lucy is not our mate," I reminded him. "At least if she were ours, if collars were about our necks, everyone would know she belonged to us. What if she leaves the planet while we attend this meeting with Dr. Helion?"

Niklas frowned. "Yes, I thought of that. However, there are more events planned for the birthing day festivities. Lucy will not leave for The Colony before the queen's celebrations are over. She has already insisted we accompany her to the royal ball."

"True. And she must please the queen," I replied, somewhat appeased but not completely. The festivities were planned to continue for two more days. Still, that didn't give us much time to woo her. Even if she stayed.

Niklas arched a brow. "The queen is her friend. She won't leave early. Lucy is loyal. We know that from her dedication to the Atlan Wulf and his family."

"Loyal. Trusted with a Warlord's family. And she's a screamer," I added, although I lowered my voice so only Niklas could hear. "When her pussy clenches as she comes..." I didn't finish that sentence, for I had to shift my cock in my pants. If I said more, I might just come in them. I was that aroused by the Earth female. "What if she meets another warrior while we are away? Chooses another for one of her Earth customs, this one-night stand? There are many honorable warriors among the palace guards."

Niklas growled, his hands curled into fists and his eyes became dark and menacing, as if we were heading into battle. Exactly the reaction I had hoped for.

"We are in agreement?" I asked. "We are keeping her?"

"She is ours."

I smiled then, relieved. "Then why are we in transport on our way to Dr. Helion? I can think of more pleasing things to do with the time."

"Duty calls."

I hated that answer. I had to hope, now that he'd agreed to make Lucy ours, that he would soon bend to less work and more pleasure.

"You wish to make her your mate," I said, ensuring I understood him correctly, although a diplomat never misspoke. "Despite the fact that we do not know her well? That dozens of other females would line up and beg to be your mate, Lord Niklas? Favorite of Prime Nial. Best friend of the most feared Prillon assassin in the universe?"

Niklas looked at me like I'd lost my mind. Perhaps I had. Lucy consumed me, every thought, every moment. "Most feared? What of Ander?"

The giant he spoke of had just entered the transport room, so I made my voice loud enough to carry. "Lord Ander? No one's afraid of him. He's too pretty."

The scarred warrior scoffed at me and clapped me on the back. Hard. "I am beautiful. It is true. My mate tells me every time she screams her pleasure on my cock."

The mate he referred to was our queen, so I wisely agreed. "Exactly." I turned back to Niklas. "He's too pretty. No one's afraid of him. They're all terrified of me."

Niklas actually smiled, the first one I'd seen on his too serious face in months. "Agreed. You are terrifying. As to Lucy, we know enough. She will be ours."

I sighed, relieved by his words. She'd propositioned us unexpectedly. After that, we'd been too occupied to talk, to strategize how we would proceed with her. "What is your plan?"

A Prillon like Niklas always had a plan, especially after a night like we'd had, when he'd allowed the lovely Lucy to be the aggressor. It was so unlike the dominant male Niklas was, but it appeared he'd been... amused by her boldness. It had certainly gotten my cock hard. More than once.

"She had her fun last night. It's my turn to take charge next. To let her know what it will be like to be claimed by Prillon warriors."

The image of Lucy, with hair the color of a sunset

over a Trion desert, submitting to Niklas, of the two of us fucking her together, collars about our necks, made me puff up with pride. The thought of our cocks buried deep in her pussy and ass as the color of our collars changed from black to dark blue while we claimed her officially, made my heart race. Made me... hope. A mate had not been what I expected to find at a palace party.

Never would I dread such an event again.

"You will collect the collars before we return to the palace?" I asked. He had to claim them from his residence. He hadn't expected to find a mate at the palace either.

Lord Ander moved to the front of the line to mount the platform. He turned to look back at us. "You two done mooning over that female? We have work to do."

I checked my ion pistol on my thigh and followed Niklas onto the transport platform. When Ander's personal guard did not follow, I looked to him for confirmation. "No personal guard?"

Ander shook his head. "No. Dr. Helion has called in an entire squadron of guards."

"Why?" Niklas asked.

"There was an incident involving the Nexus unit last night."

"An incident? Is that why a new meeting has been added to my schedule tomorrow?"

"Yes." Ander provided no additional details, so I waited for Niklas to do the clever thing and get some answers out of the male.

"The meeting appeared on my schedule, but there is no location listed."

"Helion and Nial agreed not to register the location in any official records."

Fuck. Only Ander could get away with calling the prime by his given name. Well, Ander and the queen. No doubt she could call Prime Nial by any name she wished. As Lucy could summon me...

Something in Ander's tone caught Niklas's attention. "What? Why? Exactly where are we going tomorrow?"

Ander checked his own weapon, and I realized he was wearing armor, not the tunic he would wear if this were a political meeting. "We will be transporting to Sector 437."

Fuck. "Battlegroup Karter's sector?" That area was a hotbed of Hive activity. "I need more weapons."

That made Ander chuckle. "No. You don't. We're having a private meeting on a cargo ship in Commander Karter's sector."

"With whom?" Niklas did not like surprises. He was used to knowing everything about everyone.

"A human female and her mate."

Lord Ander took out three more ion blasters, checked their charges before putting them away and adjusted the thigh-length blade strapped to his right side. I didn't ask. It wasn't my place. And Niklas was apparently too distracted by mention of a secret meeting with a human female to ask on my behalf. But Ander's concern heightened mine. Exactly what kind of *incident* had the Nexus unit caused?

Between one heartbeat and the next I dismissed the question from my mind. I did not care. I cared about one thing right now. One. And she had red hair, green eyes and liked to sleep between us.

The transport pad buzzed with building energy, and I leaned in close to make sure Niklas could hear me over the noise.

I was much more interested in what would happen when we returned from this errand than in pestering Ander for answers he clearly had no intention of providing. The idea of including Lucy in our future made my heart race and my cock harden. "This is no time for misunderstanding, Niklas. If you don't want Lucy, I will claim her and ask another to be my second. She is perfect. I will not give her up." She was bold, passionate, affectionate—she'd curled around me and clung for hours as she slept—loyal to her friends, admired by one of the most famous Warlords in the war, trusted by Governor Maxim of The Colony, beautiful, and alone.

Just like we were.

"No need to threaten me, Sambor. She is ours. Tonight she will know our intentions."

"Tonight we will be at IC Command and every Prillon warrior in the palace will be pursuing our mate."

"No. I have made arrangements to return early. We will not leave our mate unclaimed."

"Excellent." I nodded, not for the first time relieved that he'd thought ten steps ahead, as usual. "Tonight." I was pleased to know I was fighting for more than just the Coalition now, that I would be protecting more than just Niklas. I was fighting for a mate. Her name was Lucy. She was ours. She didn't know it yet, but I looked forward to seeing her face when she found out.

Preferably with my cock buried deep and her gasps of pleasure filling the room along with her surprise.

With that, the hum of the transport and the electrical zing pulled us from Prillon Prime and sent us to IC Command headquarters to tangle with an uncooperative Nexus unit. I hated this place. Hated war and killing, if I was being honest. But my father had told me when I was just a child that a warrior didn't choose this life, it chose him. I'd never doubted his words, but today was the first I arrived on this rock with a smile on my face.

Fuck Dr. Helion, the vice admiral and her Elite Hunter mate, Quinn, who awaited us. Fuck the Hive Nexus unit buried in a holding cell somewhere deep in the rock beneath our feet. I didn't want to worry about the Nexus unit, Dr. Helion, or what the fuck we were going to do if we couldn't stop the Hive expansion into Coalition space. All that analysis and worry? That was Niklas's job. I'd watch his back and I'd think of the warm, pliant female who now slept, sated and filled with our cum. Her body knew she was ours. It was time for her mind to accept that fact.

Next time we fucked our female, we would know every emotion, every desire, every want and need and fear coursing through her head. The collars would bind us three into one and make clear to every male on Prillon Prime that she was under our protection. Our care.

That we had claimed her and would kill for the right to court her.

Once our collar was around her neck, we could begin to win her heart. Her trust. I wanted to see more in her eyes than lust. I wanted... more. I wanted it so badly I didn't dare think the word.

By the gods, the collars would be next.

ucy, The Palace, Prillon Prime

"I'D TELL you to spill, but it seems by the look on your face that it was good," Gabriella said. She hadn't transported with us, but had shown up later. She had baby Jori on her shoulder, and she was gently patting his back although he'd been asleep for the past ten minutes.

"A look isn't enough," Caroline countered, pointing at Lindsey, then Rachel. She stabbed an odd, three-pronged fork into a piece of reddish Prillon fruit that was piled in the center of a fancy palace plate. "She has to spill. I want details. Every. Single. Detail."

I held my coffee cup up near my mouth, trying to hide my smile. Yes, the guys had put a smile on my face, but my Colony friends were amusing. Especially since I was the one who'd gotten lucky last night. More than one of my friends had brought along their kids. While there were sitters who'd watched all the children in a nearby nursery last night during the party, they were back to being parents after it was over. Like the coach turning back into a pumpkin at midnight, so did they become parents to babies and toddlers. While I had no doubt they had sex, and lots of it, I had to guess it was always quick, quiet and they had one ear listening for interruptions. It wasn't the same thing as what I'd gotten the night before.

Oh, they'd had that kind of wild, unhurried, *all night* fuck-fest before they had wild little toddlers running around, but now it was my turn.

Mine.

My pussy practically grinned with glee.

And ached because being with Prillons meant two cocks. Two voracious lovers. Lovers who had stamina that had me rethinking my half-hearted workout routine.

I blinked, realized they were staring at me. Waiting. I set my cup down. "Sorry. Zoned out for a minute."

"I bet. Obviously those two fucked the brains right out of you," Rachel added, waggling her eyebrows. She took a drink of juice from a tall, fluted glass, then wiped her mouth with a cloth napkin. She tried, I could tell she did, but the gut-busting laughter followed almost immediately. She was mated to two Prillon warriors herself. I had no doubt that of all the ladies here, those with Prillon mates would know exactly what kind of loving I'd had last night. All night.

I sighed, let it out, thought of all the ways Sam and Nik had taken me.

"Yeah," I replied.

Rachel squealed, then stifled it when she looked to Jori. Caroline grinned and Lindsey silently clapped like a cheerleader.

A servant brought over another pot of coffee, set it on the round table between us, then left as silently as he'd arrived. We were outside on a terrace several floors up. The sun was blocked by an arbor covered in vines with lush leaves and lavender flowers. It was a warm day, and the yoga pants and T-shirt I wore—God bless the S-Gen machine to make comfy casual clothes—weren't break-fast-at-the-palace worthy, but the girls had dragged me from bed first, then out of my room, and this was the best I had been able to pull off. No makeup, hair in a sloppy bun. We were in the guest quarters, which had its own terrace and dining room. The Colony ladies had gathered here instead of going to the formal dining room for brunch. Since Rachel and Jessica were so close, Jessica had joined us.

I'd been intimidated by her until she'd giggled and wiggled her eyebrows at me with the rest of them. Then I remembered the most important thing about her: she was mated to two Prillon warriors as well. The collar around her neck, Rachel's and Kristin's too, reminded me that they had permanent mates.

What would I do with two males like Nik and Sam if I had them every day? Every night?

Good God. I'd never walk right again.

Hand shaking, I set my cup down on the table and tried to compose myself. I knew my redhead's complexion was giving away just as much, if not more, than my guilty expression. I thought of some of the things I'd said last night. Things I'd asked them to do to me.

Jeez. I'd been totally out of control.

Leaning back, I tried to look much more innocent than I was feeling, suddenly reluctant to kiss and tell. What I'd shared with Nik and Sam felt... special, somehow. I knew it wasn't. Knew I was fooling myself. But even if it wasn't special or true love or matched mating, it was personal. Very, very personal.

We sat at a round table. The chairs had fancy cushions colored a dark, Deston family red. They matched the collar around Queen Jessica's neck exactly. The entire palace, and this space, would be in some fancy Earth interior design magazine. It made my one-bedroom living quarters on The Colony seem drab and plain. I felt as if we were at some fancy hotel with statues and flowers and ornately decorated walls and ceilings. The tables were inlaid in something that looked like marble in geometric designs that must have taken months to create. I had the feeling they had been handcrafted, not ordered on the S-Gen machines. Lush draperies and carpets, all decorated with splashes of the royal red, filled every room that was designed for comfort. The other rooms? The grand hallways? The ballroom we'd been in last night? The floors glittered like marble with a rainbow of colors I had to assume represented all the major families of Prillon

Prime. Red. Green. Multiple shades of blue. Bronze. Copper. Gold.

I was walking through a fantasy land surrounded by guards. Governor's mates. Queens and kings—like the rulers of Viken, who we'd passed in the corridor.

And little old me. Somehow my sex life had become the topic of utmost importance.

"Shouldn't we be talking about queen business? Or the war? Or something important?" I asked.

Queen Jessica smiled. "Not on my birthday."

Rachel shook her head. "Your birthday was yesterday."

Jessica snorted. "My birthday this year lasts four days. If you argue with me, I'll have Nial and Ander throw you in the dungeon."

"Do you actually have a dungeon?" Rachel asked, eyes wide.

Jessica looked confused. "I don't know, actually. Maybe we should all take a field trip after brunch and find out. That would make all the guys happy."

A round of nervous laughter followed her announcement, but I wasn't excited about the prospect. I had enough craziness going on while I was here. I didn't need to go looking for any more trouble than I was already in. And my heart told me I was in a lot.

Rachel, of course, noticed my lack of enthusiasm. "Okay, woman. Spill. You got sexed up last night. We all know you did. So what's the problem? Why don't you look happy about it?"

I picked at a piece of bread, something like a croissant

but with fruit inside. "I expected to be... dominated. Ordered about. Taken."

All of them frowned at my words. "I've never met either of them, but they seemed like perfectly normal, powerful and bossy Prillons to me," Lindsey said.

Caroline nodded.

"I met Niklas once. He came to The Colony for a meeting with Maxim and the other governors of the planet." Rachel waved her hand. "It was way before you showed up. He seemed nice. Diplomatic. Hot, but it seems like every alien is hot."

Everyone agreed. I couldn't deny it, but I thought Nik and Sam were the hottest of them all. So did my pussy. I shifted in my chair.

"It was a fun night. I'll never forget it. I definitely got what I came for."

The girls stared at me, then giggled.

Yeah, I'd definitely gotten what I'd come for. Double the cocks, double the hands, double the mouths. There had to be some mathematical formula tied to those numbers and the total orgasms I'd had.

"They left though. I mean, I'd made it very clear it was just while I was here, this... fling. But I didn't expect to wake up alone, you know? I guess when I said it was a one-night stand, they took me literally."

"They didn't want to leave you. They had to." We all turned at Jessica's words. She shifted in her chair and settled back with her arms crossed. "We just said we didn't want to talk about war, but our mates never stop fighting, do they?"

Rachel sighed. "No, they don't."

"From the hickey I see on your neck, they weren't fighting the Hive last night," Rachel said, using her fork to point at the queen's neck.

Jessica blushed and absently ran her fingers over her dark red collar. "Fine, I got a little sidetracked with Nial this morning after Ander left." She looked to me. "So... Ambassador Niklas and Captain Sambor. I saw you leave the party with them last night."

It was my turn to flush hotly. "I'm so sorry. I know that it was your party and all, but—"

She set her hand on my wrist. "Girlfriend, those two are fine. F.I.N.E. I don't blame you for ducking out. The way those guys danced to the Electric Slide, it was good timing. They might have gotten hurt, and then what would have happened?"

"No dick for Lucky Lucy," Caroline singsonged.

I put my hands over my face.

"I didn't mean to make you upset," Jessica said, her words soft. "Lindsey told me about your plan."

I gave Lindsey a death glare. Really? She'd told the freaking queen of Prillon Prime that I was on the prowl and wanted to find some hot, single warriors to hook up with?

"I also heard how protective Warlord Wulf is over you," she added. "So I totally get it. And you picked two hotties to have a good time with."

"Thanks. They were... good."

She smiled and arched a brow like a wicked queen, not the sweet one she seemed to be. "Just good?"

They were all staring at me now. Waiting. Damn it.

There went my redheaded complexion again. I was probably the color of a ripe tomato.

"Okay. Fine. They were incredible. Rocked my world. Three times. No, four."

"If you can't remember, then they were doing it right!" Rachel added.

"Yes. They were doing it right. And then they left." I brought it up because I was still bothered by the fact that I'd fallen asleep nestled between two of the hottest warriors ever to have existed. I'd been warm, safe, sated and happier than in the past few months. Probably years. And then? Nothing. Which was exactly what I'd told them I wanted. It was what I'd wanted when I transported here. I had a family on The Colony. Olivia and Wulf and the kids. I loved Tanner and Emma like they were my own. Olivia was a sister in every way that counted. I couldn't leave them. Could I?

No.

So why was I so upset? I woke up alone in bed every day. Usually it didn't bother me. In fact, I wasn't much for sharing the covers. And I kicked, or so I'd been told by an old boyfriend years ago. But he'd been a bit of an asshole, so maybe my subconscious had been acting out its dark fantasies when I was asleep.

I blinked, realized I'd been staring into space again as Jessica leaned forward. "Like I said, they didn't leave because they were done with you. Ander said he was headed to another meeting with the IC commander and Ambassador Niklas. Since Sambor is his guard, no doubt he is with them."

I set my fork down, my appetite gone. "Are they in

danger? Why aren't you worried if one of your mates is meeting with the Intelligence Core? Those guys are serious business." In fact, one of the top guys, a doctor named Helion, had recently tangled with Mikki and her two Prillon mates.

Mikki was sitting next to Lindsey across the table, and I shrugged my apology. "Sorry to bring up the IC. I know you aren't a big fan."

Mikki shrugged right back. She'd been quiet until now, her perma-smile in place and her long, sleek black hair looking too perfect for morning brunch. I wanted to get my hands on it and style it, but the simple cut suited her. She had been a world-class surfer on Earth, and the surfer attitude hadn't disappeared once she'd arrived on The Colony. In fact, she seemed even more relaxed. But then she'd found her place in this world, teaching swimming and diving lessons at the Coalition Fleet's academy. When she was on The Colony, she was helping her mate, Dr. Surnen, catalog and explore new species and plants from oceans on other worlds. She was useful.

I was just... me. Nothing special, really. I cut hair sometimes, and occasionally helped with makeup. Most of the time I helped Olivia with Tanner and Emma. So not sexy. Or exciting. Boring, really. Why would a high Prillon lord who was one of the Prime's top ambassadors want to tie himself to me when he could hop in that testing chair and get a perfectly matched female from any world in the Coalition? Not attach himself for life to a random, horny woman who'd practically tripped and fallen into his arms doing a country line dance.

Sheesh. I was a mess.

Jessica squeezed my arm, apparently misreading my distress. "Ander will be fine. So will your two guys. Besides, all three of them have reason to fight hard and get back here."

When I frowned, she added, "You. Niklas and Sambor aren't going to let you go."

Well, she was wrong there. "Yes, they will. I'm not an Interstellar Bride. And I leave in less than two days. I told them from the beginning. I'm game for another night of fun, but then I'm going home. And this time the fun can't start until *after* the ball's over." I didn't want to offend her by ducking out of all the birthday party events.

Rachel and Jessica exchanged looks. So did Mikki and Kristin. Caroline just stared at me with a growing smile on her face.

"No way, girlfriend," Caroline said. "No way."

"What? What am I missing?"

"When Jessica said they're not going to let you go, she means they're going to keep you. Make you theirs," Rachel clarified. "Put a collar on your neck."

"Claim you," Linsdey added.

My mouth fell open, my heart pounded in my chest and my hand flew to my bare neck, massaging the soft— and very unclaimed—skin. "No way. I'm just an unmated hairdresser."

Jessica turned as a woman came to join us. I recognized her only because she'd had the three Viken hotties trailing behind when I'd first seen her yesterday, and because she had red hair like me. It was Leah, queen of Viken. *Three mates!* Yet she was alone.

Jessica stood and hugged her, then made introductions. I was thankful I wasn't the only one who was new to her. She wore the traditional Viken dress, but her red hair was long down her back and she had no makeup on her face, not that she needed any. She was beautiful.

"We were talking about Lucy's new Prillon hotties."

Leah looked to me. "You're mated to Prillons?" Her gaze dropped to my neck, and she frowned in obvious confusion.

"Unmated," I replied, as I took a sip of my water. "That's me."

"She had a fling with two Prillon warriors last night," Caroline clarified.

"Answer this, oh Queen of Viken," Jessica began, sounding all formal, although by the look on her face, she was amused. "A gorgeous redhead rocks two Prillons' worlds last night. What are her chances of going back to The Colony?"

"Alone? Or for a visit with a collar around her neck?" Leah asked.

"Alone," Jessica, Lindsey, Rachel and Caroline all said at the same time.

"No chance." Leah hadn't even taken a second to think about her answer. Not. One. Second. And there was no hint of laughter in her gaze. No joking. No hope that she was having a bit of fun at my expense.

"What?" I asked, stunned. Then I realized who I was talking to. "Sorry. I'm not sure if I should call you Your Majesty or what."

The queen cocked her head to the side. "If you call me that, I'll be really pissed. I'm Leah to my friends, and that includes you." She shrugged her slim shoulders. "Besides, we redheads have to stick together. I think you might be the only other ginger in twenty sectors. Even up in a bun like that, the curls are perfect. What do you use?"

"Lucy's a stylist," Rachel said. "Did everyone's hair and makeup last night for the party."

I rolled my eyes, plucked a wayward curl. "You wouldn't know it by looking at me now."

Leah pursed her lips. "If you're styling everyone for the ball tomorrow night, I want in. I wonder if the kings would like me with a nose ring."

I couldn't help but smile. Leah was cool, and she did have crazy red hair like mine, although hers was sleek and styled and my curls were messy and tangled as if a guy had gripped it while he took me from behind. Which had happened. The fact that she wanted hair advice proved she was just being nice.

"Those Prillons are going to want to keep you." Leah said, going back to her original statement.

The others nodded. Jessica, God help me, gave me a death glare. The queen of Prillon Prime was glaring at me like I'd done something wrong. "Prillon warriors, especially those two, don't fuck around, Lucy. They don't. If they took you to bed, I'd say there is a ninety-nine percent chance one or both of them had already decided to keep you before you left the party last night."

"What?" No. No way. "I tripped and fell during the line dance."

"Let me guess, one of them caught you before you

even hit the floor." Rachel's smile seemed to be contagious, because everyone at the table was smiling but me.

"Yes."

"Which one caught you?" Jessica asked, as she oh-so-innocently popped a piece of fruit into her mouth.

"Nik."

"Oh, so it's Nik already, is it? Not Lord Niklas? Or Ambassador Niklas? Or even his full name? It's Nik?"

"I..." I had no answer. It did seem a bit informal.

Jessica kept at me. "Let me guess—you call Captain Sambor, one of the most decorated warriors on Prillon Prime and one of the most skilled assassins Nial has, just plain old Sam?"

"Sam's an assassin? I thought he was Nik's bodyguard?"

Queen Jessica raised a brow like I was a five-year-old who hadn't done her homework. "Lord Niklas Lorvar has been serving as an ambassador for more than a decade. His cousin is a battlegroup commander. His family is ancient and highly respected. He does not mess around with every female that crosses his path. And Captain Sambor Treval? He's adored by every Prillon warrior in the fleet. He's practically a legend. He's feared by our enemies. He's taken down Rogue 5 leaders, smugglers, illegal weapons dealers and more Hive than I can count. The list of awards and military skills certifications after his name in the files is so long I stopped reading. He's not just Ambassador Niklas's bodyguard. He's Niklas's weapon. They've got the good cop–bad cop thing down to an art form. They're not playthings, Lucy."

Great. Now I'd pissed off the queen of the planet. And

this was not Las Vegas. Seemed what happened here might not stay here after all. And somehow I was the player? The jerk? The heartless asshole? Me? Back home I wouldn't even squish a spider. I'd catch them and set them loose outside.

Shit. I was in deep trouble. "I'm sorry. I didn't mean to... I don't even know why they'd be interested in me then. A fling, sure. But forever? I do hair for a living."

"You do more than that," Jessica said. "Rachel told me you wanted to open a spa."

"On Earth," I clarified. "The Colony is not really the place. I can't see any of those guys going in for a facial. There's not enough women there."

"There are on Prillon Prime," Jessica said, those eyebrows going up and down again.

"Viken, too," Leah added, then looked at Jessica. "I haven't had a spa day since Earth. You know, I'd come to Prillon Prime for a girls' spa day. And if two queens showed up..."

"It would be the hottest place on the planet!" Rachel added.

I was quiet, bit my lip and thought. "The idea is a good one, and I can read between the lines. You're saying all this because you think Nik and Sam want to claim me. I say it's just a fling."

After everything I'd learned about them, I was even more certain the match was uneven.

For once everyone at the table seemed out of words. Everyone but Jessica. "Just be careful, okay? They aren't human, Lucy. They don't think like humans. Not when it comes to claiming a mate."

A guard dressed in black camo from head to toe, toting a nasty looking weapon, appeared at the door and cleared his throat. He was golden, like Sambor, and serious as hell. "My queen, Prime Nial has requested your presence at once. There has been word from Styx Legion. And Commander Zeus is on the comms."

Jessica stood like her chair was on fire. She took a step, then looked back over her shoulder at me. "They're good guys, Lucy. Really good guys. Don't break their hearts, okay?"

I nodded as she left. Around me, the others speculated what the message from Styx Legion on Rogue 5 might be about. Apparently, the leader—named Styx—had taken a human woman for his mate as well. And this Commander Zeus? He was the only half-human, half-Prillon commander in the Coalition Fleet. Mikki told us he'd been in contact with her mate, Dr. Surnen, multiple times because somehow he'd taken a human woman captive. A human woman who was contaminated and still connected to the Hive. And Dr. Surnen was one of the foremost experts on removal and destruction of Hive integrations.

A human woman turned into a Hive, then captured by a Coalition battlegroup. Alive?

Fuck me. And I thought I had problems. I felt like I was pretty darn petty.

By the numbers, there weren't very many of us Earth girls out here in space, but we sure did seem to be everywhere, right in the thick of this war.

Under the table, Lindsey took my hand and squeezed. "It'll work itself out, Lucy. Don't worry."

"I'm not worried." I lied like my life depended on it, because somehow this fling had turned serious on me, and the males I'd taken to my bed weren't even here. How had this happened? And what the hell was I going to do now?

__iklas, Prillon Prime, The Palace

I WORRIED Ander would notice or care that I hadn't been the most... diplomatic with Helion, not that he never deserved such poor treatment. The Prillon was an asshole, and my job was to be nice to assholes. Dr. Helion, despite his well-earned reputation for being diffi-cult to deal with, was invaluable to the entire Coalition. No one could do what he did and remain unaffected.

The male needed a mate more than anyone I knew. However, I had no idea if there existed a Prillon male insane enough to be his second. Gods help them if the day ever arrived when Helion took the Interstellar Brides Program matching test. Gods help all three of them.

That was assuming there was a female out there, somewhere in this universe, tough enough—or insane enough—to put up with that male. On more than one occasion, I had seriously doubted even the Brides Program could find a match for him.

Watching him argue with Vice Admiral Niobe had made me bite back a smile more than once.

That female was not to be fucked with. The Elite Hunter standing at her back—Quinn, her mate—didn't bother holding his amusement in check. But watching the fire burning behind Helion's gaze, I decided there was, indeed, a perfect female out there for him. I'd place odds that the female in question would be from Earth.

These human females were a force to be reckoned with. Including mine.

Lucy. I could not wait to return to her, place my collar around her neck and make my intentions known.

I'd enjoyed being taken by her, claimed by her last night. Although I doubted Lucy realized that's what she'd been doing.

But I knew. So had Sambor. We'd accepted her claim with every touch. She was ours now.

Thank fuck Ander grew tired of the meeting as well. We weren't getting anywhere. Helion had yet to have a breakthrough with the Nexus unit. It had been months with no progress. There would be no resolution today.

"Gwendolyn Fernandez is the only one left who might be able to communicate with that thing," Helion said. "With her own time with the Hive, her integrations..."

"We know about her," Niobe said. "But she's rogue. No one has seen her in months. She's a ghost."

Ander sighed. "She was on The Colony. Friends with my mate and the other females from Earth. I asked the queen to try to make contact through her network of human females."

Niobe looked at Ander with wide eyes. "You did what?"

"It is my mate's birthing day celebrations. The females from The Colony are all at the palace."

"Yes, we will be at the ball tomorrow night," Niobe said, flicking a glance at her mate.

"I should be with her now, not here." He all but glared at Helion. "If getting to Gwen through the ladies is all we need, then we can end this meeting now. I would prefer to avoid Jessica's wrath."

Niobe laughed as her mate muttered, "I can imagine."

Ander wrapped his knuckles on the desk. "Helion, I asked Jessica and Lady Rone to contact Gwen. We have a meeting set for tomorrow in Sector 437 if she accepts. Until then, we're done here." He didn't wait for an answer, just nodded at the guards and left the room, leaving Dr. Helion stuttering in shock.

"Lord Ander! Wait one moment. I need more details."

"Tomorrow, Helion." Ander didn't even look back.

"You going to the royal ball?" I asked, looking at Dr. Helion.

"I have work to do." With that, he took off after Ander. The sight made me smile. He would have no luck whatsoever. None.

Sambor and I nodded to the others, then followed him out.

I'd been distracted during the meeting with Helion, thinking of Lucy. Everything about her, especially the unsure smile that had spread across her face when I'd bumped into her on the dance floor. That one, small curve of her lips and I'd been done for.

I'd been ready to toss her over my shoulder and carry her back to my quarters near the palace. Then she'd propositioned me. *Us.* An unmated Earth female had boldly requested Sambor and myself give her orgasms.

As if that had ever been in question. Then she'd led us back to her room by tugging on invisible chains like we were submissive Trion females. We'd proven for hours that we were far from female and had exactly what she needed to be satisfied. Over and over again.

Her cries of pleasure, the way her pussy had clenched and dripped all over our cocks, her nails as they dug into my back. The way she writhed as she rode Sambor to her own satisfaction.

She'd used us so beautifully. And we'd allowed her to possess us, to take whatever she wanted, from our taste to the seed from our cocks.

Fuck, had we allowed her. I would have given her the blood from my veins last night.

Tonight Sambor and I would pledge her our lives. Our honor. Our protection. Tonight I would place the collar around her neck and we would know her mind, her heart, her desires.

During a moment of clarity, I'd sent a message ahead to one of my staff to deliver the collars to the transport room on Prillon Prime, and they'd been waiting for me, two dark Lorvar family blue collars, and one much smaller black collar for our new mate. I didn't want to waste a moment before going to Lucy.

Now, after transporting from IC, I stood before a

locked door at the palace and gripped the collars in my hand, looked down at them as I had over the years. I'd waited for this moment when I would approach the female to be my mate and stake my claim. *Our* claim, for Sambor had waited equally as long.

He shifted his weight from foot to foot, was just as distracted and eager. Almost ravenous for Lucy from Earth.

I looked to him. He nodded. I rapped my knuckles on Lucy's door. Beside me, he took a deep breath. Exhaled.

"I told you I don't want to do karaoke with—" Lucy's words cut off when she saw us, the door bouncing off its well-oiled hinges and bumping into her hand, which was still sticking out.

Her green eyes were wide, and her mouth hung open. Clearly she hadn't expected us. I watched her thoughts flit across her face before she put her hand to her head, then stepped back and slammed the door in our faces.

Sambor looked to me.

I frowned, knocked again. "Lucy."

"Um... come back later!" she called, her voice muffled by the thick door.

"We are not coming back," I said. She may have been in charge the night before, but not now. "Open the door, please."

"I will if you come back later."

"What is wrong, Lucy? Are you hurt?" Sambor asked.

"No. I'm fine. It's just..."

I stared at Sambor and he shrugged.

"Open the door, Lucy, or your ass will have my handprint when you come next."

She moaned.

"You are hurt. Move away from the door, Lucy. I am opening it to see to your safety." Sambor's words were laced with the same dominance as mine, but his held concern too. So much for me being the diplomatic one.

He turned the knob and slowly opened the door, cautious not to bump our mate. Sambor stepped in first and scooped her into his arms. I followed him over to the bed, where he sat, placing her in his lap. His hands roved over her body, and I looked but could find no injury.

"What hurts?" I asked.

She looked to me. "Nothing hurts."

"Why did you moan?" Sambor asked as she swatted his hands away from her breasts. The way the nipples pebbled beneath her simple white shirt didn't indicate they were injured. What had she done while we'd been gone?

She closed her eyes. "God, could this be any more embarrassing?"

"No injury is shameful," Sambor said, lifting her up as if she were a doll so she stood before him. He spun her around in a circle, checking for something broken or bleeding.

"I moaned because Nik's words were hot."

Sambor stilled.

My cock was instantly hard. "You want to be spanked."

She looked over her shoulder at me and blushed a bright pink.

"Well, a good-girl spanking."

"A good-girl spanking," Sambor repeated. "You slammed the door in our faces first. Why?"

"Why?" she said, tossing her hands up in the air. "You're all gorgeous in your uniform and Prillon leadership clothes, and I've got my hair up in a sloppy bun. I have no makeup on, and I'm wearing yoga pants and a T-shirt."

I looked her over from the wild hair on top of her head to her toes. She was covered in freckles, golden dots all over her face and arms. Sam must have noticed the same thing as he hooked a finger into the round collar of her shirt and tugged it down an inch or so, exposing a few more of them.

"I do not know what yoga is," I replied absently, intrigued by her gorgeous marks. I hadn't seen them on her face and chest the night before when we'd gotten her bare.

Why would she hide such rare marks?

"It's an exercise regimen that made me flexible enough to have my knees by my ears last night."

My mind shifted to fucking her with my hands on her thighs, pushing her legs up and back. She'd been able to achieve remarkable positions with ease.

Sambor's eyes widened, and his hands went to her hips, slid down the tight fabric that hid none of her curves.

"You are beautiful, mate," I said. I remembered her words from the night before when she'd told us about her profession, how she wanted to make females feel confident. That their appearance affected their happiness. I'd said it was a mate's job to make her feel attractive and confident. It was true. She was gorgeous, and I would never stop telling her that.

She laughed and turned to face me, although she didn't appear amused. "I look like I should have six cats and drink wine while I knit tea cozies."

I could understand and communicate with members of every planet in the Coalition, but Lucy had me stumped. I had no idea what to say to that, so I just repeated myself. "You are beautiful, mate."

She huffed, then started coughing. "What did you say?"

Sambor stroked her back.

"I need to say it again?" I asked.

"You called me 'mate.'"

"He did," Sambor clarified. "Not once but twice."

Her pink tongue darted out and licked her lips. "I'm not your mate."

"Not yet." I held up the open collars. "You will be."

She sputtered, then stepped back, although I didn't let her go far. "You guys are crazy! I can't be your mate."

"Why not?" Sam asked.

"This was supposed to be a one-night stand. No matter how good the sex is, a fling's not the basis for a true match."

"You chose us last night out of all the males at the party," I stated.

She ran her hand over her hair, glanced at the ceiling as if it understood her better than we did. "Most of the guys there are mated. I don't do married men. Or whatever they're called in space."

"That makes you honorable," Sam stated.

She set her hands on her hips and glared at him. "Honor isn't enough to spend your life with someone. *Two* someones." She waved her hand in my direction.

"The attraction, the connection between us was instant," I said.

She laughed. "You believe in love at first sight?"

I gave a slight shrug, looked her over and considered. "I do not doubt the bond between us."

"I don't even know you!" she shouted, tossing up her hands. She walked across the room, then spun around and came back our way, pacing as if she were on guard.

"I know enough to give you my collar," I said, my words heavy. I'd never said them to anyone before, and I never would again. Lucy was mine. No other female would compare.

"I know you well enough to also wear a mating collar," Sam added.

"What's your favorite color? Do you like crunchy or smooth peanut butter? God, are you allergic to nuts? What about meat, do you eat it? Do you live in a house? What about you, Sam? Where do you live? I figured I'd marry one guy, but two is a struggle. I mean, do you even put the seat down? How am I going to survive two guys leaving the seat up?"

"What seat?"

"The toilet." She was pulling at her hair, clearly on the verge of panic. "Oh shit. I forgot. Those implant things. Do you guys even pee anymore? They don't on The Colony. It's so weird. Everything is so weird."

I stepped into her path and set my hands on her shoulders. "Slow down."

Her green eyes narrowed as she looked up at me. "Don't tell me to slow down. I've got an alien who wants to put a collar around my neck, and I don't know how he feels about me except the sex. Sex is not a relationship."

I held up the three collars, their lengths dangling from my fist. "Put the collar on and you'll know everything. You have friends mated to Prillons. Lady Rone, Dr. Surnen's mate."

"Mikki."

"Yes, the brilliant female who discovered the Hive's water transport machines."

"Yeah, they told me about them, how they can feel each other, know each other's emotions, if they're hurt or scared."

I nodded. "That's right. You'll know all of that, how Sambor and I feel about you, if you put on my collar. All your questions will be answered."

"Just like that? The little things are what's important."

I bent at the waist so we were eye level. "Is knowing my favorite color truly important to a strong match?"

"Yes."

It *was* important to know the nuances and character traits of another person. Especially one from a planet so different. Cultural differences alone were a huge impact on perspective, which was the issue at hand right now.

I lifted my hand and curled a strand of her soft hair around my finger. "It's red." I tugged her close and kissed her eyelid. "And green."

She pursed her lips, but she wasn't pacing anymore. Progress.

"Everyone you mentioned was matched through the

Brides Program. They were tested and the match is almost perfect. None of them had to worry about leaving the cap off the toothpaste. I mean, you're an ambassador and I was told about all your achievements as a fighter." She pointed at Sambor. "You two are amazing. I'm... just me."

"You are rare, not only in person, but in being unmated and no longer on Earth. Do you deny the connection between us? Is your pussy not wet for us?"

"My pussy should not be in charge of the rest of my life," she grumbled.

"Put the collar on, Lucy. All will be revealed. Trust us, one more time."

She rolled her eyes but turned her head to Sambor, who was still sitting on the side of the bed. He nodded. "I wish to share my every thought with you. How I feel. I wish to *know* you."

She crossed her arms over her chest, the act was not one of defiance but more like a wall of protection. "If I put the collar on, we're not going to be instantly mated, right?"

Something loosened in my chest at her words, the fact that she was considering it.

"An official claiming, where the collar changes from black to dark blue, only occurs when your mates take you together."

Sambor stood, came over and moved behind her so she was between us, just as she would be when we claimed her. Not *if*.

When.

"And only when you consent to be ours, Lucy." He

leaned down and kissed the side of her neck as he had last night. "When you say yes, I will fuck your ass," Sambor said, tugging the neckline of her shirt to the side so he could kiss her lower on the shoulder.

"I will fuck your pussy. We will claim you together. You will bring us together, make us one. Only then, when you accept us both into your body, when you say the ritual words, only then will you be truly and completely ours."

Sam licked up her neck. "And we will be yours. Why did you cover your freckles?"

She tilted her head, trying to avoid him, but he would not have it. "I'm covered in them. They're ugly."

I dropped the collars to the floor, freeing my right hand. While I would not treat something so sacred with such disregard at other times, Lucy was more important than the collars. "Ah, mate. All of you is beautiful." With my fingers in the hem of her shirt, I slowly lifted it up her body. Sambor leaned back so I could tug it over her head.

She wore nothing beneath, and she crossed her arms over her chest.

"What happened to the brave and fierce woman from last night?" Sambor asked.

She looked anywhere but at us. I wished she wore the collars so we could understand.

"She covered her imperfections with makeup."

"Why would you do that?" I asked.

She looked up at me, eyes wide. "Because they're awful!"

I reached down and grabbed the collars again. "Put this on. Let us understand."

It was obvious she had issues with body perception and vanity.

"Did a male on Earth reject you because of them?"

She swallowed hard and still wouldn't meet our eyes.

"That would be good news," Sambor said.

Lucy spun on her heel to face him, her hands still covering her chest. "That's mean."

He stroked a finger over her cheek that I knew to be silky soft. "It is good news because that means you are unclaimed, that there has been no male worthy of you. Until now. Until us. We see *you,* Lucy."

"Let us wear the collars and all will be clear. Trust me," I said, using my most diplomatic tone. In all the years I'd been in my role, this was the most crucial conversation of my life.

"Fine. But no claiming. No, 'Whoops, your ass fell on my dick while Nik's got his in your vagina.'"

I couldn't help but laugh. "You doubt our honor?"

She blushed and finally met my eyes. "No, you're right. I apologize. You wouldn't trap me." She sighed. "Fine. The collars. But I'm taking it off if it doesn't work out. And I'm leaving after the ball, so..."

It would work out and she wouldn't be leaving without her collar being dark blue and her body claimed as ours. If I said that aloud, it would push her too far. Although she would know the truth once the collar was about her neck, but at least then she'd be wearing it. She would know the truth. Words were one thing. They could be fake or twisted to make people happy. I was a diplomat, a master of that.

The collars didn't lie. When I picked them back up,

handed one to Sambor and quickly put mine about my neck first, then helped Lucy on with hers, no words would be needed.

Everything we were and would be together would become clear.

7

HOLY SHIT. I had to be the only woman on Earth whose one-night stand wanted forever. Oh yeah, I wasn't on Earth. All those women who'd successfully had their fun and forgotten completely about the guy had done just that. *Slept with a normal guy.* I'd had sex with an alien. A bossy Prillon warrior.

Not just one, but two.

Two who shared a woman together. Who planned to mate and claim one forever.

I might have picked up Nik and Sam at the party, but they weren't planning on letting me go.

Not just that, they wanted me to wear a Prillon mating collar, an outward sign to anyone who saw me—them, too—that they were claimed. This... fling I'd planned to have wasn't to be a secret.

They wanted everyone to know about us.

About whatever this was.

The girls had all been right. I'd brought human assumptions into bed and hadn't believed my friends when they told me this was not going to go the way I'd planned.

My pulse was at stroke point, and I had that tingly feeling in my chest. The one where someone jumped out and shouted boo and made my adrenaline dump into my bloodstream all at once.

On Earth I'd dreamed of a guy who'd sweep me off my feet, one where there was an instant connection and I just *knew* he was the one. On The Colony, I watched all the couples who'd been matched through the Brides Program and *knew* they were perfect for each other.

Now I had two Prillon hotties with huge cocks and skilled hands and mouths who *knew* I was the one for them.

What was wrong with me?

Dreaming was one thing, reality quite another.

Yet...

I'd met them during the Electric Slide. They were horrible dancers but definitely made up for it in other ways. I'd have seen them at the party. I'd have approached them. I'd have propositioned them.

Why? Because I'd been drawn to them. Then and now.

I touched the collar about my neck, looked to Sam, who closed his collar about his neck. I knew from the girls who had them about the feelings that came from them and—

"Holy shit."

I reached out and grabbed Nik's arm, the powerful sensations coming from the collar overwhelming.

"Shh," Nik said. "Breathe. It is intense at first, feeling me and Sam, sensing our need for you, our desire to make you ours."

I looked up at Nik through my lashes, feeling how much he liked my exposed breasts, and Sam's arousal and eagerness to fuck me.

"Good girl."

My mind flashed to what Nik had said earlier, about a *good-girl spanking*, and I got hot all over.

Nik smiled when Sam groaned. "See? We're just as overwhelmed by you, by your thoughts and desires."

Sam's big hands settled on my bare waist, slid down, hooking into the tops of my yoga pants on the way and baring me to them.

"You wear no undergarments when you dress this way," Sam commented, and I *felt* as well as heard how much he liked it.

"No. Who wants to wear a bra or panties when you're by yourself?" I asked, lifting my feet so he could tug the stretchy material free.

"Or with your mates," Nik added.

I stood between them bare while they were fully clothed. Sam's hands caressed back up my legs to cup the cheeks of my bottom. Then he spanked me. Lightly, but I startled. The sting was minor, but the heat that followed made me moan. I turned to him.

His pale eyes and wicked grin were lethal to my brain and any effort I had to resist them.

They wanted me. The collars clued me in. So did the bulges in their black pants. The look in their gazes.

"A good-girl spanking," he murmured, then stepped back.

From one second to the next, Nik bent at the waist and tossed me over his shoulder, carrying me to my bed. He dropped me upon it and I bounced.

They loomed over me, standing at the foot of the massive bed. I hadn't thought about it the night before, but now I knew why the beds were so big. They could fit two Prillons and their mate.

"We should give you a bad-girl spanking for doubting us."

"I didn't doubt—"

Nik shook his head slowly and held up his hand. "I know your thoughts. Your feelings, mate. Lying doesn't work, even with yourself."

He was right, and I bit my lip.

"Last night you were in control. It is my turn now," Nik stated.

A thrill shot through me, and the growl that ripped from Sam's chest meant he felt it. Nik looked to Sam. "Strip and get up in bed. Let's see how our mate feels about being restrained."

Restrained? I thought those from Trion were the kinky ones.

Sam either took orders well or didn't care about being bossed around when it meant he was going to get laid, because he had his uniform off in record time. He crawled up the bed, loomed over me on all fours and kissed me, then flopped onto his back. Adjusting the pillows behind his head, he settled beside me.

Scooping me up with his impressive arms, he placed me in front of him, facing away. I was settled between his parted legs, his hard cock at my back.

His arms came beneath mine and grasped the insides of my thighs and pulled them apart, then over his sturdy thighs. When he bent his knees up, mine went with them.

"Oh my God," I breathed. My legs couldn't have been parted any wider without pain. I was bare, my pussy lips open to both Nik's heated gaze and the cool air. I envisioned Nik climbing the bed toward me, settling his mouth over my clit and making me come as Sam held me in place, maybe, someday, as he filled me from behind.

The images in my head, my reaction to feeling so open, so vulnerable...

And they knew I liked it because... the collars.

"Put your hands behind my neck," Sam said, nuzzling the side of my head.

Lifting my arms, I interlaced my fingers as he'd said. My back arched, and my breasts thrust up.

"From here, I can see all your freckles. Ah, ah," he warned when I started to relax my hands. "I shall spend my life counting them all. Licking each and every one."

"Sam," I breathed.

All this time, Nik watched as he shed his clothes until he stood at the foot of the bed, naked, pumping his cock.

I felt his pleasure. God, it was insane. I *felt* the pleasure Nik was getting from masturbating. I felt his satisfaction at seeing me restrained. Not in any kind of binding, but by Sam's hold. By Sam's words. I felt Nik's contentment that Sam and I followed his orders, that we were both his.

As if he had read my mind, Nik crawled up the bed to kiss me. Not on the mouth, but on my pussy, licking up the seam, then using his thumbs to part me and do it all over again.

I bucked at the pleasure. Sam groaned. Nik growled.

"These collars are too much," I said on a laugh, then a moan. The sound of my pleasure sent a jolt of lust through both of my mates and, through the collars, back to me. I nearly came, my hips bucking as I tugged on Sam's hair. "It's insane."

Sam's hands cupped my breasts, his thumbs brushing over my nipples, each stroke sending a spiral of heat to where Nik's lips were locked onto my clit. "Nik." I didn't know what I wanted.

No, that was a lie. I knew exactly what I wanted, what I needed: more.

Instead Nik stopped and stared. Watched Sam's hands cup my breasts, his eyes going molten as he slipped a finger inside my wet pussy and felt it clamp down and release with every tug of Sam's fingers on my nipples. It was erotic. I was beyond embarrassed. I couldn't be, not when their admiration and need blazed through my body like a wildfire from the collars.

"Do you doubt our desire for you?" Nik asked, glancing up at me from between my thighs. I looked down the line of his back, saw his taut, firm ass and wanted to unlink my fingers and squeeze it.

I shook my head against Sam's chest.

"Do you doubt our need to please you?" Sam asked as Nik got busy again, adding a second finger inside me as he flicked my clit with his tongue. "Not just when we fuck you, but with everything we do?"

I arched my back more as Sam tugged on my hard nipples. My skin bloomed with sweat. My thighs clenched. "It's too much, too... oh my God, I'm going to come."

My shout didn't slow Nik down; rather he applied himself more. I came seconds later. Their ruthless assault was to prove a point. An incredible point that the collars only made everything more intense. Amplified. More powerful.

When I stopped screaming, Nik lifted his head, wiped his slick mouth with the back of his hand, then came over me. His mouth was on mine, and I tasted myself. I felt the satisfaction he found in pleasing me. His need to be buried inside me. I didn't want to deny him that. It was what I wanted, too.

Sam's hands settled on my upper arms, holding them, as if he didn't want me to touch Nik. Nik looked behind me, over my head and nodded slightly to some silent question Sam had asked of him. Moments later Sam aligned his cock at my entrance and slid home, buried deep in my pussy from behind, my legs still held open wide as he lifted his hips and pumped into me from below.

I gasped at the feel. He was big, thick, long. He filled me completely. After the night before, I should have been used to taking him, but I wasn't. I clenched and squeezed him, and the feel of it was unlike anything I'd known before them.

Hovering over us both, Nik watched my face as if every movement I made was of vital importance. "Fuck her, Sam. Go deep. She needs more."

Sam thrust up inside me, hard.

"Ahhh!" I cried out as another orgasm built. How had he known? The collars were for emotions, right? He couldn't actually read my mind?

Nik placed his hands on my inner thighs and stroked my skin with a lover's touch as Sam moved inside me. The gentleness, the tickling softness in contrast with the rough fucking had me panting. Keening. Overwhelmed. I had no words. No thoughts.

Nothing of me was left. I was theirs.

"Life with us will always be like this," Sam said as he thrust deep, fucked me thoroughly. Nik held me securely. I could do nothing but surrender. My pleasure built up their pleasure. Their pleasure escalated mine. "Niklas on one side of you, me on the other, protecting you, taking care of you. Just think, my cock could be buried in your ass right now. We could both fill you at the same time."

I moaned and could do nothing but feel, and with the collars, it was incredible. I sensed how much Sam wanted to fulfill his words, to take my ass.

The thought of it pushed me to the edge. There was no way I could hold off another orgasm. It was just too much. I came, this time on a silent cry, Sam following me. My pleasure brought on his, and he thrust hard, held himself buried as I milked the cum from him.

He pulled out, and Nik pulled my hands from about Sam's neck.

Nik hooked an arm at my waist and rolled onto his back, taking me with him so I was on top, straddling him.

Kissing me, he ran a hand up and down my sweaty back, stroked my bottom. I felt Sam move over us, and it was Nik who widened my legs so Sam could get between, this time from behind.

Sam's grip at my hip tugging me up was all that he needed to sink two fingers deep into my pussy.

Nik broke the kiss but watched me, took in every nuance of my face as Sam stroked my swollen core, pulling his fingers out slowly, rubbing the slick wetness over my ass.

I felt anticipation build in Nik as Sam's touch rekindled the fire inside me until I was squirming, not caring who fucked me, who filled me. I just *needed.*

When I wanted to scream at one of them to *do something*, Nik shifted my hips and lined his cock up at my core. I didn't wait, slamming down onto his hard cock with a cry of satisfaction as he filled me up. Stretched me. Gave me what I craved.

Nik pulled me down on top of his chest, which put my ass back up into the air where Sam waited behind me.

Nik's thrusts slowed as Sam ran his thumb through the wetness he'd spread to my ass, then pressed the tip of it inside. His touch was slow, gentle but insistent. With Nik's huge cock stretching me open, the added pressure of Sam's thumb in my ass was like an electric shock.

"It's too much," I breathed, my nipples chafing against Nik's bare chest. I'd done ass play before, but not with two guys. I sensed Sam's satisfaction at how I was taking a bit of both of them at the same time. Nik's cock was much larger than Sam's thumb, and I wasn't sure how both of their cocks would fit inside me. I'd seen porn, knew it was possible, never considered it for myself. Until now. Until Sam painted a naughty picture in my head. Until his thumb was sparking nerves I didn't even know I had.

When my body settled, I shifted, rubbing my clit against Nik's stomach, clenching my muscles around both of them. I was stuffed full of my lovers, but I knew they wanted to give me more. A lot more.

The pleasure was already so intense, I wasn't sure I would survive more.

Nik shook his head, stroked my damp hair back from my face. "It's real. It's us. Feel it. Know us."

Nik slipped his hand between our bodies to stroke my clit as Sam slowly worked his thumb into my ass. Stretching me. Making me burn.

Sam's intense pleasure washed over me like whiskey in my blood as he played with my ass, filling me, pulling out, rubbing around the edges, getting me ready for more.

For him. For his cock. Soon I would be between them, filled by both. Held by both. Fucked and claimed.

Nik moved, rocking his hips beneath me just enough to make me want to scream as Sam kept slowly fucking my ass. Sam leaned down and placed a kiss on my spine. My hip. My bottom. His lips on my skin, the scent of Nik's body where my cheek was pressed to his chest, the heat. Their need. God, there was no lying about their desire for me. Their lust. Their appreciation.

I felt beautiful. Wild. Like a completely different woman, one without doubts or inhibitions. I was raw and untamed and out of control. Without their touch anchoring me, I feared I wouldn't exist at all, the cells in my body barely holding themselves together. I was stardust. Energy.

Lust.

"Come, Lucy. Come now. Know you are our mate."

I came at his command, clenching and squeezing around Nik's cock and Sam's thumb, my body instinctively reacting to the need I felt from Nik for my submission, at Sam's complete and total control, his intensity as he prepared me. Opened me. Stretched me for his claiming.

For that was what they would do.

Claim me.

Bind me to them forever.

Fuck me together. Fill me with two cocks as I was now filled with two minds. Two desires. Two alien males with relentless physical needs and an unwavering desire for me.

Me. Lucy. Their—

"Mate." The word burst from me. I'd meant to say Nik's name, or just yell or scream or groan. But I'd finished my thought aloud, and Nik's reaction was like a nuclear explosion inside my mind.

His fingers dug into my hips as he locked me to him. Sam came again, his hot seed splashing on my lower back. His release triggered another orgasm in me. Nik growled as the culmination of the sensations we all felt through the collars went from coherent lust to something wilder. He'd held himself off until both Sam and I found release, until our feelings were built layer upon layer and they burst through our minds like a flash flood breaking a dam.

Nik came on a shout, filling me with his seed. I came again with him, my pussy eager to spasm and pulse, so close to the edge for so long the orgasm never seemed to stop.

I'd been right in my words. Adding Nik and Sam's pleasure to my own had been too much. The last I remembered before I passed out was Nik and Sam gently cleaning me before I was tucked snuggly between them. Right where I was supposed to be.

8

Niklas, Coalition Transport Ship, Location Unknown

Lord Ander, Sambor and I materialized standing next to one another, the transport beacon on my chest buzzing with energy as I scanned the cargo area, making sure that Gwen and her mate, Makarios from Rogue 5, had not yet arrived.

The room was empty except for Dr. Helion, who held an ion pistol pointed in our direction. We were safe on a Coalition ship and in a rarely used section for this fairly clandestine meeting, but he still was clearly wary. He didn't trust anyone, even us, whom he'd been expecting. Gods, he'd been the one who wanted this meeting. While Ander had been able to make it happen, the location wasn't IC Command, and Helion lacked control. He seemed to hate that.

Fascinating. I had never seen this side of him, and I

was suddenly very curious as to who had inspired such emotion.

"As I said yesterday, my mate was trying to help arrange this meeting," Ander said. "She was successful. Although I am grateful, I would prefer to be in her bed, not standing in a cold cargo hold in deep space." This was the second day in a row our duties to the Coalition had taken him from her side during her birthing day celebrations.

I could relate since Sambor and I had been pulled from Lucy's bed as well. Normally I lived for my work. This was the first time the thrill in my blood was directed at going home rather than going out on the next mission.

"Gwendolyn Fernandez of Earth and Makarios of Kronos Legion will arrive shortly." Dr. Helion settled his weapon back into its holster on his thigh.

Good. Because just behind me, Sambor had his own weapon leveled at Helion... just in case. Sambor liked a good laugh, but when it came to fighting, he was ruthless. Which was just one of the reasons I'd chosen him so long ago to be my second. He protected me with expert precision, and he would protect Lucy the same way.

Our mate did not lack bravery, but hers was of a different sort. She had the courage to leave her planet, and not for a mate. She had explained she'd gone to The Colony because her friend, Olivia, had been mated and cuffed by Atlan Wulf. Lucy lived there without having a mate—or mates—of her own. Still, she'd chosen to go out into the unknown, to another world for the family she loved. Olivia and her niece and nephew.

I wanted that fierce love directed at us. To earn Lucy's

love, I needed to get back to her. "How did a human female end up with a mate from Kronos Legion?" I asked.

"That's irrelevant." Dr. Helion snorted. "And human? Gwen? Hardly. She might have been human once. Now she is a weapon."

Standing slightly behind me, watching my back as always, Sambor shifted. Normally I would have read his agitation at the doctor's words from that one small movement. With the addition of the mating collars, his dislike of Helion added to my disgust at the doctor's choice of words. The idea of him speaking of a human female so similar to our mate in such a clinical way had me disliking him all the more. I wondered if her Rogue 5 mate knew of Helion's thoughts.

"A human female? A weapon? How is that possible? I've seen them handle themselves with a ReCon Unit, but alone? They are small and weak, Doctor. How is a defenseless human female dangerous enough to have you nervously pulling your ion blaster?" I asked, wanting to see what he would say next. He was far from a diplomat. Perhaps that was why Lord Ander had ensured I was in attendance.

The doctor paced the room, clearly nervous. "She single-handedly destroyed a Nexus unit on The Colony. I tried to track her down, but she and that fucking hybrid mate of hers stole a ship with advanced stealth tech. They have eluded me completely."

"What type of hybrid?" I knew all members of the legions on Rogue 5 were part Hyperion. Their fangs and aggression made them dangerous enemies.

"Forsian." Dr. Helion glanced from me to Sambor,

then Ander. "In addition to that, he has full Hive integrations. That's why you three are here." His gaze lingered on Ander's bulk next to me, then on Sambor's weapon. I, too, could fight like a demon if provoked. I'd thought we were here for diplomatic reasons. To negotiate some kind of deal.

Apparently we were here to be Helion's muscle against a hybrid Forsian cyborg.

Fuck. Not a fight I wanted to be in. I had much more pleasurable things I could be doing.

"So they eluded you but agreed when Queen Jessica asked for her help?" I used years of practice to keep my amusement from showing in my expression. The idea that a human female had irritated the most pragmatic and ruthless intelligence operative I knew entertained me, despite the fact that her mate was a scary bastard from Rogue 5.

Helion scowled.

Ander ran a hand over the back of his neck. "Exactly. I spoke to my mate, who spoke to Lady Rone."

I sorted through names. "Rachel? Governor Maxim's mate?"

Ander nodded. "Yes. She knew Gwen before. They were friends during Gwen's time on The Colony before she and her mate went rogue."

"She went rogue?"

"I told you, she and that Forsian of hers wiped out a group of Hive, including a Nexus unit, stole a ship, and haven't been seen since," Helion snapped.

"She sounds fucking amazing to me," Sambor offered,

and I knew he was purposely irritating Helion. We had so few opportunities to do so.

"The human will not respond to my request for information or assistance," Helion complained.

"Why not? Did you make her angry? Betray her trust?" I looked at Ander, wide-eyed, knowing Helion would never answer such a question.

Ander gave me a look, then sighed. "The females do not trust easily. And getting my mate involved"—he gave Helion a dark look—"during her birthing day celebrations was the fastest way I could think of to get this hunt of yours over with."

"We need her. I need to know what she knows. What she can do." Helion, as usual, was completely unapologetic.

Ander sighed and shrugged as if to say, *See what I mean?* Aloud he asked me and Sambor, "Do you wish to spend time with Helion and his Hive Nexus unit for a third day in a row?"

I didn't respond because I knew it was rhetorical. None of us wanted to be here when we had warm, willing females waiting for us back on Prillon Prime.

"Trust me, Lord Maxim is not thrilled to have his mate involved in issues like this, but Lady Rone was able to get Gwen to come here. If, and I mean if, *here* was a cargo ship in Sector 437, protected by Commander Karter's battlegroup, where there was no chance Helion would try to capture *her* as well."

Helion's clenched jaw was all the indication I needed to know that had been his hope. It seemed the Earth female was smart—or very familiar with the IC commander.

"Girl talk, I've heard it's called," Helion replied as if it was sour in his mouth.

"You are speaking of my mate and your *queen*. She and Lady Rone achieved overnight what you have yet to accomplish. Tread carefully, Doctor." Lord Ander spoke quietly, but his words carried the weight not just of Queen Jessica's mate, but of a warrior who was battle scarred and very protective of his female, as all Prillon warriors should be. And he was here with this asshole rather than at the palace with her.

As usual for the doctor, he did not apologize but continued on. "The human females have disproportionately affected this war." The speed of his pacing increased. "They seem uniquely adaptable and highly creative. Their minds can handle the effects of the Hive implants and still retain control. It's remarkable. The brain bleeds are a problem, but with time I'm sure I can solve that obstacle. I simply need more of the females to work with."

The doctor was obviously thinking aloud. Still I felt my ire rise at the thought of the doctor placing Hive implants in any human's brain, especially my Lucy's. "Don't even think about it, Helion."

I spoke for *all* Earth females, not just mine.

Sambor's rage rivaled my own, the psychic link between our collars making me speak a bit more forcefully than I had intended. I did not lose my composure. Ever.

Helion stopped midstep and looked up at me with

surprise. When his gaze dropped to the mating collar around my neck, he sighed. "Fuck. Not you, too."

Ander shocked me by chuckling. I had never heard the scarred male laugh.

"A human?" Helion asked.

"Yes."

He stared as if waiting for me to give him more information about Lucy, but I was not inclined to provide details to a male who had just spoken of experimenting on human females and their brains. He would know nothing of her.

"I am happy for you, Niklas," he said, sharing the smallest shred of courtesy. "Sambor is your second?"

"Yes." Sambor answered for himself, which was unusual. Normally he remained silent and watchful as I conducted business. But I felt his need through the collars to make Helion aware of the danger of messing with our female.

"Good for you." He paced again, his impatience growing. "Where is that female?"

"In a hurry, Doctor?" Lord Ander asked, sarcasm lacing his words. "Please note, whatever outcome this meeting has, we are adjourned for the next three days. My mate's generosity in helping you has caused me to be away from her. The same can be said for Niklas and Sambor and their new mate. You will need to plumb your own depths to be the diplomat all on your own, Helion."

Helion's cheeks mottled red at Lord Ander's scolding, but I didn't blame Ander. Gods, I wished I'd said the words myself. I felt Sambor's satisfaction.

Dr. Helion turned away, fists clenched and shoulders

stiff, as we all felt the disturbance of energy in the room. "They are arriving."

I couldn't decide who was more pleased by that.

Sambor took his weapon out and leveled it at an area of visual disturbance on the other side of the cargo hold. The space was large, and Ander had said he'd given our visitors precise coordinates.

When the two guests materialized, I was surprised to find the female looked completely human. And lovely. Long black hair fell to her waist. She had darker skin than my Lucy, and her eyes were a deep brown similar to some of the other human females I had seen. Next to her, Makarios of Kronos was massive, as I'd expected. What I had not imagined was the apparent lack of concern on his part for his female. She stood out in the open next to him, unprotected should Sambor decide to take a shot. Helion's weapon was at the ready, and I knew Ander and his contingency of guards with him were armed.

"Dr. Helion, I presume." The female spoke first, looking to the IC commander. The uniform had been an easy giveaway. The massive male next to her glared, much like Ander, but larger even than an Atlan. I stared, not able to resist the urge to inspect him thoroughly. He had dark hair, dark eyes and fangs. A solid foot taller than any Atlan I'd ever met. I was surprised not to see any Hive integrations on his body.

He snapped his fangs at me, and I grinned back, unrepentant. "I was told you both came by way of The Colony. But I do not see any integrations." I was trolling for information, not sure any would be forthcoming, but I would take my chances. They were both fascinating. I believed

Makarios of Kronos's anger was focused more on Helion than the rest of us. I didn't blame him. It seemed many were inconvenienced this day because of him.

The female spoke for him, probably because the hulking male did not look inclined to humor my curiosity. "Oh, he's got 'em. Shoulder. Hip. Thigh. Knee. A lot of microscopic stuff. He was strong before. Now he can rip his way through a Hive ship's outer hull with his bare hands. Can't you, baby?"

His grin was the only proof I needed. I felt Sambor's shock at her words coupled with my own. That kind of strength simply wasn't possible.

I supposed the surprise showed on my face, because Makarios spoke with pride. "My mate is stronger." His laughter made light of his joke.

Assuming it *was* a joke. I wasn't sure. I looked at Sambor, the question on my face and, I had no doubt, communicated clearly though our collars. He shrugged and Helion was quick to take advantage of the small break in conversation.

"Gwendolyn Fernandez of Earth," Helion spoke quickly, his voice like sharp beats in the room.

She nodded and held out her right hand. "You can call me Gwen."

Helion stared at the proffered hand, so I moved around him and closer to the female. I'd been around enough humans to recognize the peace offering of a handshake, as they called it. This was my role, to keep her from transporting right back out of here before we'd gained any knowledge from her.

I placed my right hand in hers and bent low over our

joined hands. "I am Ambassador Niklas Lorvar of Prillon Prime."

She waited patiently for me to let go of her hand, and I did so quickly, not eager to upset her mate. I released her and straightened She grinned and the look reminded me of Rachel's face when she was teasing Governor Maxim or Captain Ryston. Or even the sly twist of her lips just as Lucy did with me. "I know who you are. Rachel gave me the 411 about the party the other night... that you two left early. Congratulations."

I had no idea what the numbers meant, but I understood the context, the fact that she knew Lucy had taken us back to her room.

"This is Mak." She thumbed over her shoulder, casually introducing her mate.

I inclined my chin to the male but did not offer to touch him. I was not a fool. "Makarios of Kronos. I am honored to meet you."

He crossed his arms and stared at me. "I don't like this, so make it quick. We're here because Gwen and Rachel are friends." He switched his attention to Helion. "And that's the *only* reason." He looked behind me. "You must be Ander?"

A nod of Ander's head was his only response.

"And you?" Makarios was looking at Sambor now.

"I am Sambor Treval. I am the ambassador's private guard and his second."

Makarios gave Ander's guards—who'd stood at attention and silent behind him—a quick glance, but their role was clear.

Sam's words made Gwen smile. "I've heard about you, too, Sam. Nice to meet you guys."

Sam? Had she just called him Sam? "How do you know of Lucy's name for him?" I asked, which was completely out of character and off topic. It was not my job to veer into personal matters, especially not my own, but I couldn't help it.

That made Gwen laugh. "Oh, you boys are funny. I know all about you two and Lucy. From what I've heard, she's a sweetheart, so you better take good care of her."

How the fuck did this female who hunted Hive on the other side of the galaxy know about the mate I'd just met and had yet to officially claim?

My shock must have shown on my face, because Dr. Helion chuckled. "I did warn you. The human females have some kind of secret communication network. They keep secrets from us." He glared at Gwen, but the face she made was another I recognized from watching Lucy every moment since we'd met, and from dealing with Queen Jessica the last few years. Annoyance. She was *annoyed* with the most powerful male in the Intelligence Core. Not upset or intimidated. Annoyed.

"Why am I here, Helion? Rachel said you've got a Nexus unit locked up. Good for you for capturing one, but I heard all the credit goes to Vice Admiral Niobe. Another Earth woman, right?" She didn't wait for him to answer. "What do you want from me? Let's get this show on the road and get these guys back to the party."

My thoughts exactly.

Helion actually huffed. "I need to know how you are finding and targeting the Nexus units. I need to know exactly how you are taking them out. You have destroyed two that I know of. How?"

She crossed her arms and shook her head. "Nope. Nothing I can say would help you. Just stay out of our way so we can get the job done. The one *you* can't."

"I can't do that."

Now her annoyance turned to aggression, and I wisely stepped back to watch the interaction play out. There were times for diplomacy, and this wasn't one. I had never seen anyone refuse Helion anything.

This should be interesting.

9

*S*ambor

I SHOULD HAVE BEEN SHOCKED at the female's sharp words. Instead I found myself amused. Wearing the collars was interesting, even without Lucy here. I assumed Niklas would also find the female entertaining. Now I *knew* he did. His amusement enhanced mine. And this human female? So much fire. Passion. Just like our Lucy. Makarios was a lucky man. When Niklas and I got off this battleship and back in Lucy's bed, we would be, too.

"Listen, Doc," Gwen continued. "I know you sent that stupid probe to try to track our ship."

"I—"

"No." She raised her hand, palm out, toward his face. He was so shocked he actually stopped speaking. "No. You are not going to stand here and lie to me. I know it was you. Or someone under your command. Whatever. You aren't going to order me around like I'm one of your soldiers. I'm not. But I'm on your side. Be grateful and leave Mak and me alone to do our thing."

"And what, exactly, is your thing?" Helion asked, a brow raised as if he were in control here. "I have no clear indication that you are, indeed, on our side."

"We are here, and you are not dead," Makarios interjected.

"That means nothing," Helion snapped.

I disagreed. Looking at Makarios, and assuming what he said about the female's strength was true, the fact that we were all still alive meant *everything.*

"I see time hasn't changed you, Doc. You're still an ass."

Oh fuck. I knew that look. The human female was losing patience with the doctor. I crossed my arms over my chest and leaned against the wall to watch and enjoy. I had no doubt, probably due to my bias in the human female's favor, that she would not attack Helion, no matter how much he provoked her.

Niklas referred to the doctor as a necessary evil. He was very good at what he did. Loyal to Prillon Prime and the Coalition to a fault. Ruthless and merciless when dealing with our enemies.

Didn't mean I enjoyed Helion's company, especially today. Apparently Gwen had come to the same conclusion, and Niklas's amusement increased, the link through our collars calming me even more than his demeanor usually did, which was saying a lot.

Fucking Niklas Lorvar was ice. Or at least I'd always assumed. Since placing these mating collars around our necks with Lucy, I'd learned a lot about him. Primary fact was that the calm, icy demeanor was a complete facade.

"Let's go, Mak." Gwen took a step back, and the Forsian cyborg moved with her.

Helion moved forward and reached out to grab Gwen's arm, to stop her.

Mak's huge hand surrounded Helion's fist faster than I could blink. Fuck. Those Hive integrations were no joke. Not only was he massive, he was fast. "Do not."

"My apologies." Helion shook off the Forsian's hold and moved back several steps. Wise move. Idiot. One did *not* physically paw at anyone's mate. Not if one wanted to keep one's hand—or head—attached to his body. "I am trying to protect my people, Gwen. I have been fighting this war for years. You are unique. You have exposed a weakness in the Hive structure we never knew existed. I am merely asking for information."

Gwen paused, her head tilted to the side as if considering his sincerity. "Look, I am not being difficult. You can't help me unless you get captured, integrated, then escape with your mind intact. Even if they happened to give you the same integrations I have, you would have to find a mate to anchor you mentally so you could immerse yourself in their minds to draw them to you. And..." Her pause was long, as if she considered her words carefully. "The Hive made me what I am. They wanted me to become a mate to one of them to see if the *upgrades* would be inherited in any children I produced."

I had not been aware of this, of what she'd endured. To be a mate to the Hive? To have children with them as an experiment? She was not my mate and I wanted to hold her, to soothe the ache that I knew kept her motivated at her task. It explained so much about her motivation. And Makarios's.

"You are a male. You would not be given the same... integrations they gave me," she continued. "You would not be what I am."

"What are you?" His eagerness was apparent. *This* was the question he had most wanted to ask.

"I am what they are."

Helion's body tightened with every vague answer she provided. "And what is that, exactly?" he asked, a snap in his voice.

She shrugged again, and I hid a grin as Helion scowled at her. "I don't know."

"That is not helpful," he countered. For the first time ever, I saw him flustered, running a hand over the back of his neck.

"It's the truth."

"So they chose you because you were female?"

She shrugged. "Chose? Doubtful, but when I was captured, they saw... opportunity. They've integrated millions of females from other worlds, including humans. Maybe billions since this war began. I don't know why they did this to me specifically."

I knew why, but I would not speak it with Helion in the room.

She was human. Adaptable. Passionate. Able to

tolerate the technology and still think independently. A soldier first. Everything Helion had just said about human females replayed in my mind, followed immediately by a fierce and desperate need to return to Lucy and make sure she was safe. We were too far away for me to sense her through the collars, and that absence made me... anxious.

While Gwen seemed well, she was different because of what the Hive had done to her. Her life course had been redirected. Decided by another. I would not have that happen to Lucy.

The obsessive worry was new, and not at all welcome.

Obviously annoyed, Niklas glanced at me over his shoulder with a clear message to knock off the emotions. It was impossible.

I looked around. I wasn't the only male in this room. All of us—perhaps besides Helion—felt something toward the human female bickering with the IC commander. Fuck. Sympathy, admiration, pride. I had to get control of myself. I was jeopardizing the mission and Niklas' effectiveness by being distracted. But I could not stop thinking about our mate. Her soft skin. Her hot, wet core wrapped around my cock. Her lips. Her scent. The sounds she made when we touched her and made her come over and over and over.

Another annoyed look and a flash of irritation through the collars.

Ion cannons. Forsian hybrids. Fangs. Hive Scouts. Battle screams. War. All of it filled my head, and I used it to gain control over my emotions.

Niklas turned back to face Gwen as I focused on

something other than our beautiful, eager female. Her red curls. Her green eyes. The way her emotions rolled through my mind and went straight to my cock. Her anger? Happiness? Contentment?

Her mind had touched mine, and my body responded with *need.*

Ander spoke. "My lady, the Nexus unit has been transported here and is on this ship specifically for this meeting. We have tried to interrogate him for months with no success. We were hoping you might be able to speak to him, get him to talk. If you can, break open his mind. The doctor is hoping to gain a tactical advantage in the war."

I blinked at Ander, processed what that meant. He'd planned to have Gwen come here, to neutral territory. Once that was done, he must have forced Helion to relocate his Hive prisoner to this ship just for her.

Niklas hadn't known either, and based on the swirling feelings coming through the collar, he'd picked up on the plan.

Helion gave up all pretense of being in control of this meeting and asked, politely, for Gwen's help. "It was our hope you could... connect with him as no one else has."

Makarios growled as if Helion had asked his mate to slit her own throat.

Niklas apparently picked up on the threat from her mate as well. "Gwen, it was not our intention to place you in harm's way. We have tried everything we know to force the Nexus unit to answer our questions, yet he is impervious to our attempts."

And by *attempts* Niklas meant everything we could

throw at the Hive leader. Starvation. Torture of all kinds. Kindness. Logic. Puzzles. The Nexus unit was... unique. And Gwen was already shaking her head.

"Sorry, Nik." She had now used both of our pet names, the names only Lucy had bestowed upon us, and I knew Helion was right about one thing—these human females did communicate with one another somehow. "I'm not trying to be difficult. I'm not. There is nothing I can do except kill him, and to do that I'd have to rip off his head."

"You will not touch it," Makarios growled, and she twisted to place a hand on his arm.

"I know. Don't worry, Mak. I think they want to keep it alive."

"Idiots."

Well, the big male didn't mince words. I hid my chuckle as the warrior in me felt a solid kinship with the big brute. I was no diplomat like Niklas, nor a doctor like Helion who wanted to learn and pick the Nexus apart and study him. I destroyed my enemies. That kept my life simple.

"I need the Nexus unit alive," Dr. Helion confirmed.

"I'm sorry. I can't tell you how they made me what I am. I have no idea why they chose me instead of some other female. I can tell you that I can hear them, that they are naturally drawn to me."

"They fucking track her like Elite Everian Hunters." Mak, clearly unhappy with the fact, talked over the top of her.

"When I get close, I lure one in. They think I'm one of

them. Safe. They are arrogant. They think they can control me. Use me."

"But they can't?" I asked.

"No. When I merge my mind with theirs, Mak is always there, waiting for me. He's in my mind, too. He keeps me sane and brings me back. Somehow our integrations and our mating have connected us so that I can lure them in without losing my mind. I use myself as bait, and then we kill it."

"Why do you not interrogate them first?" Helion asked.

"Trying to talk to them is a waste of time. Their minds aren't like ours, Doc. They're—" She seemed to be searching for words. "They're empty, like an abyss. They consume. I can't explain it, but he's not going to talk to me. I can leave, or I can kill him."

"You sound so sure," I said. "Have you ever tried to question one of them?"

Gwen looked to me, then to Niklas, whose gaze was serious but held respect as well. The look she gave us was not at all similar to the one she gave Helion. "No. Shit." She glanced over her shoulder at Makarios, who inclined his chin to his mate as if to say it was her choice. She sighed. "Fine. I'll try. But we'll probably end up killing it."

"Do not," Helion ordered.

Makarios grunted as if Dr. Helion's preferences were no longer of any concern.

I couldn't help but offer her a small smile, completely out of character for an ambassador's personal guard.

Niklas made a sound of affirmation, a pseudo-grunt.

"I'm sure Dr. Helion is pleased by your offer of assistance."

Everyone looked to Helion, whose lips were in a thin line as he nodded once. Perhaps he was afraid to open his mouth and ruin it all by pissing off Gwen. It was a possibility.

"On one condition."

Gwen's statement had Niklas taking a step in her direction. "What is this condition?"

"You, you and you." She pointed at me, Niklas and Ander. "The guards, too. I believe you were all at Jessica's party the other night."

I bowed my head slightly in confirmation.

"You'll do the Electric Slide for me. Here. Now. Or no deal." She lifted her arm and tapped a button on the comm unit there. The strange music we'd all heard at the party wafted into the small space as she grinned, completely unrepentant.

"What are you demanding, female?" Helion had his hands folded in front of himself, probably to make sure he didn't forget himself and reach for Gwen again. We all knew Makarios would not tolerate a second attempt to touch his mate.

Her smile was pure mischief. "You too, Doc. You're a smart guy. I'm sure they can teach you the steps."

"Steps? I do not even know what this... Electric Slide is. Is it some kind of ionization process? What steps?" For once Helion had no idea about something, and the fact that it was a ridiculous Earth dance that had him stumped actually made me happy.

She looked up at me, then Ander. "Well, Lord Ander,

general and all around badass. Are we doing this or what?"

"We are not."

I almost sighed with relief when Ander refused Gwen's request with a raised hand and a very blatant no. I expected her to argue, but she surprised me by bursting with laughter. Next to her, Makarios seemed as confused as Dr. Helion. She set her hand on her hip. "Fine. Just kidding. But man, that would have totally gone viral."

"Viral? Are you harboring an infectious agent?" Helion pulled a ReGen wand from somewhere in his uniform and took a step toward Gwen. Makarios moved faster, blocking his path.

Gwen wrapped her arm around her mate's and tugged gently. "It's okay, Mak. I was messing with them."

Makarios stopped advancing, but he did not move aside to allow Helion access. Gwen, however, stepped around him. "Okay, Doc. Where is this blue bastard? Let's go get into his head."

"Thank you." Helion put his ReGen wand away and took two steps toward the door. "He is being contained in an electromagnetic cell on the level below us."

"Blocking his transmissions?"

"Yes," Helion confirmed.

"Smart." She reached for Makarios's hand, and he gently enclosed her much smaller fist within his. It almost seemed as if the female was seeking comfort.

"Does the idea of speaking to this Nexus unit distress you?" Niklas asked for both of us. He'd seen the same action as me.

"Oh yeah," she said, glancing over her shoulder at us. "You ever been in one of their heads?"

"No."

"Trust me, they will suck you in like a black hole and you won't even want to put up a fight."

Makarios growled, his fangs extended to their full length. He was one scary monster. "He will not touch you, mate."

Gwen smiled up at him like he was her entire life. "I know. I trust you."

The Forsian hybrid pulled her to his side and looked at Helion. "Let's go, Doctor. I do not wish to linger. We are exposed on this ship."

"Yeah," Gwen added. "Any Hive within range will be curious and wish to investigate my broadcast signature."

As if on cue, the ship shuddered beneath our feet, the small cargo ship's shields perhaps taking a hit from an ion cannon.

I stiffened. So did Ander's three guards. Gods, all of us did. Immediately Ander hit his comm button. "Captain? This is Ander. Report."

The ship's pilot, a respected captain from Viken that we used most often on our IC missions, answered at once. "We are under attack. Two Hive Scout ships."

The ship shuddered again, and I slapped my hand on the wall for balance.

"Make that three," he continued. "I have more coming in on scanners. Arrival imminent. Recommend evacuation protocol. Now."

A loud boom sounded, and the ship rocked onto its side, throwing Makarios into the nearest wall, taking

Gwen with him since he'd wrapped his arms around her. I stumbled, caught myself against a support beam and reached for Niklas. He was right there next to me, and I pulled him to the beam as Ander braced himself against the opposite wall, a smear of blood on his cheek where he had hit it. He wiped at it with a sneer.

Dr. Helion hadn't moved, his feet anchored to the floor by something...

"I want a pair of those boots, Helion." Niklas's voice was more order than request. He was so fucking calm, even under attack.

Helion looked annoyed. "Fuck." He glared at Gwen. "It's you. They've followed you. How long does it take them to track you?"

She shrugged. "On Earth there's a saying. *I told you so.* It depends how close they are."

"You could have warned me about this," Helion snapped.

"When I said, 'Any Hive within range will be curious and wish to investigate my broadcast signature,' that was a warning, you dumbass."

Makarios growled at him. "You forget, this meeting was at your request, Prillon. They're here for Gwen, which isn't happening. We are leaving." With those words, he reached around Gwen and pressed a transport beacon on her shoulder. His was activated less than one second later, and the two of them disappeared.

"Gods be damned!" Helion pressed his comm. "Captain. Initiate emergency prisoner transport protocol. Get the prisoner back to Core Command now. Evacuate immediately."

"Yes, sir."

Another blast sounded and Helion looked up as the door opened. There stood an Atlan Warlord in beast mode. Fucker was massive. And angry. He reached for Helion. "Come. Now."

"Who is that?" I asked, assuming Niklas would have the answer. He generally knew more about the spies and their games than I cared to.

"Warlord Bahre. He's IC. Part of Helion's personal strike team."

Helion was still standing in place, his boots somehow locking him into position on the tilting ship. "I'm fine," he told the Atlan. "Get down there and make sure that Nexus unit makes it back to command."

The beast was not happy with the snap in Helion's voice, but he grumbled and did as he was told, disappearing into the corridor. The door slid closed behind him.

Helion looked at the two of us and Ander. "Get off this ship. We will have to reschedule."

Reschedule? Like we didn't realize this meeting was over.

With that, he activated his own transport beacon and vanished.

I looked at Niklas. "Get out of here."

"Ander first." Niklas looked at Lord Ander, Queen Jessica's mate, Prime Nial's best friend and second, and a general in the Coalition Fleet. I agreed. We could not leave him behind. His guards flanked him, but they didn't give the orders. They would stay and fight, offer the general protection.

"Get the fuck out of here, Ander," Niklas ordered.

Ander scowled but gave us a nod and tapped his transport beacon, his body partially translucent as a massive explosion rocked the ship. All at once the inner walls crumpled, the pressure in my ears was instant and excruciating as the air was sucked out of the cargo hold, taking Niklas and I with it.

10

*L*ucy, *Personal Quarters, The Colony*

"Honey, wake up."

I sniffed and rubbed my cheek into the soft pillow. It smelled like Sam, and I smiled, remembering all we'd done the night before. He might be Nik's second, but he was impressive himself. Everything about him, right down to his cock. I ached in ways and places I'd never expected. Pulling the blankets around my shoulders, I rolled over, reached for Nik, who also had an impressive cock and knew how to use it, but found nothing but an empty bed.

"Lucy."

The deep voice didn't belong to either Sam or Nik. My eyes flew open. I was stunned there was another guy in my room, a guy who did not belong here, who was definitely *not* mine.

Kneeling by my bed was Jessica, her face close, our noses nearly touching. With her was Ander, who stood tall beside her, arms crossed. He was in the same black battle armor Sam usually wore. His face was smeared with dirt and... was that dried blood?

I tugged the bedding up higher to ensure my nakedness was covered. "What's up?"

"Well, we... um..." Jessica looked to me, then away. She bit her lip, and tears filled her eyes. Then she took a deep breath and met my gaze. "Something's happened. Let's get you dressed and we'll tell you."

I looked up at Ander, whose jaw clenched as if he were trying to break rocks with his back molars. "Where are Nik and Sam?"

"That's what we want to talk about. Clothes first," she said. Her voice was so calm. Soothing, even.

"Talk now," I countered.

Ander nodded, although somewhat grudgingly.

"Something's happened," she said again. "Ander was with Sam and Nik today. They had that meeting."

I pushed up on my elbow, careful to keep myself covered. "The one with the guy from IC. They told me about it, at least what they could. The follow-up from the one yesterday. That's why they left early."

Jessica glanced at the floor, then back at me. "They were all at the meeting, and their ship was attacked. I don't know the details, but the Hive... well—"

"The ship was destroyed," Ander said.

Destroyed?

"I... I want those clothes now," I said, needing a minute, unable to process what they were telling me—or rather, *not* telling me. At least not with words. The grim look on Ander's face made my chest ache and the backs of my eyelids burn with denial.

Jessica nodded and stood, going to my closet as Ander spun on his heel, faced away to give me some privacy. She returned with a sweatshirt and yoga pants, the ones that Nik said he liked. I climbed from the bed and tugged them on as my brain processed.

The ship was destroyed? But Ander is here. He was on the ship, too. Right? So where are Nik and Sam?

I pulled my long hair from the neckline of my sweatshirt as I said, "What do you mean, it was destroyed? Blown up? Crashed? What?"

Ander darted a glance over his shoulder, then seeing me dressed, turned around. I stood so small before him in my rattiest of clothes while Jessica was dressed in her gorgeous Prillon finery, ever the queen.

I kept talking. "Where are Nik and Sam? Are they hurt? You've got blood on you. You went to the meeting, too, didn't you? Are you injured?"

Ander glanced down. "No injuries a ReGen wand won't fix."

Meaning he had been hurt but came here, to speak to me, before treating his injury.

"Then take me to Sam and Nik." If they were hurt, I wanted to see them.

Ander shook his head, his fists clenched at his sides.

"While the collar about your neck is not Lorvar blue and you are not officially Lord Niklas's mate, it is my duty to be the bearer of bad news."

My heart began to beat frantically, and I became light-headed. I had an idea of what he was going to say, yet I held my breath.

"As general in the Coalition, it is with great sadness that I share with you that this morning Niklas Lorvar and Sambor Treval were both believed killed in action when the cargo carrier they were on was attacked by multiple Hive Scout ships. External scanners on Battleship Karter registered an explosion, after which, they lost contact with the ship."

My knees gave out, and I dropped onto the bed. Stared up at Ander.

"What do you mean, they lost contact?" No. Just no. My brain refused to process the words. "You were there. What happened to them? You came back. Why didn't they come with you?"

His lips pressed into a thin line. "They insisted I leave first, placing my safety above their own."

God, that sounded exactly like something Nik and Sam would do. Damn them.

I felt a sob well up, but I fought it down with cold, hard logic. "What about escape pods? Maybe the ship crashed somewhere and they're still alive. Did they send anyone out to search for them?"

Ander bowed his head, and Jessica sat next to me, taking my hand as Ander answered my questions and more.

"The Karter sent out multiple probes to look for wreckage. They looked for hours, but there were no life signs, no comm signals. All they could find were—"

He stopped and I wanted to kick him. "Finish that sentence. What did they find?"

"Pieces of the ship. Wreckage." He shuddered and Jessica quickly wiped a tear from her cheek and I realized they were sharing emotions through their mating collars. Of course they were. The pain on Jessica's face made this all too real.

"They can't be dead." I licked my suddenly dry lips. "They were just here." I pointed at the bed.

Jessica settled closer and leaned her head against mine. Her hand squeezed my fingers, and either hers were warm or mine cold. "Honey, I know. I'm so sorry."

"Why? Why were you there? Why did they have to go? What was so damn important?" Rage built in me, and I clung to it, used it to bury the pain piercing my skull like an ice pick.

"They weren't after us," Ander explained. "We set up a meeting with a human female who has unique Hive implants. She and her mate agreed to meet with us."

"Gwen. You're talking about Gwen." I had heard of the famous human woman who had tracked and killed a Hive Nexus unit in the tunnels beneath The Colony. She'd fought like a demon in the fighting pits, too. Governor Maxim had forced her to take a mate because she had been causing so much trouble.

I'd heard the stories during my time on The Colony, and I'd secretly admired her. She sounded awesome. Like a real badass. She was the reason my guys were dead? Nothing made sense.

"If the Hive wanted Gwen, why did they blow the ship up?" I asked.

"She had already transported off. They were probably mad."

I looked up at Ander. He was scarred, obviously a warrior, but he was not integrated like Prime Nial. Like Gwen and Makarios and everyone else on The Colony.

"The Hive don't have emotions like that. They don't get angry." I'd been on The Colony long enough to have learned a thing or two. Plus I'd spent enough time with Olivia and Wulf to pick up quite a lot about his time with the Hive. I had asked questions of Wulf. Dr. Surnen. Even Braun, because he'd seemed eager for someone to listen. Mad? The Hive? "They weren't angry. I can promise you that." I thought about everything I'd heard about Gwendolyn Fernandez and the Hive and the things she could do. "Gwen doesn't need a space suit. You know that, right? They probably thought they could kill everyone on board and she'd float out into space where they could just pick her up."

"What do you mean, Gwendolyn does not need a space suit?"

I shrugged, the pain and anger warring inside me until I felt numb. "Ask Dr. Surnen."

Jessica rubbed her hand up and down my back, and her touch was making me angry for no good reason. I didn't want her touching me. I didn't want anyone touching me except Nik and Sam, and they weren't here. Weren't ever going to be here again.

I needed to be alone. I needed to process.

I needed to curl into a ball and cry, and I didn't need witnesses. I looked from Jessica to Ander and fought for control.

"I'm so glad you're all right," I told Ander. I was. Happy for him, for Prime Nial, for Jessica. In a very strange way, I was also proud of Nik and Sam. They'd protected Ander, insisted he transport away first because that was who they were. Protectors. Loyal. Perfect.

And gone.

Jessica popped up, went over to Ander and hugged him from the side. His arm went around her shoulders, and her head tucked into him. "I survived only because my guards and I initiated our transport beacons when we did, otherwise…"

"You would have been on the ship when it exploded. Just like Nik and Sam," I stated, figuring it out.

"I would have, yes."

"Then if you weren't there, you don't know if they're dead," I reasoned. "I mean, they could be alive. Injured. Maybe part of the ship blew away and they had to crash somewhere. Maybe the comms are down and we just don't know."

Ander shook his head. "They were in deep space, too far from any planet to survive the journey in such a condition. I am sorry, Lucy. There was nowhere for them to go."

"They're really dead," I said, finishing what he couldn't.

He nodded.

Jessica moved back to me, hugged me. "Honey, I'm so sorry."

I didn't know how I was supposed to feel. I'd only known Nik and Sam for two days. Heck, less than that. I'd only arrived on Prillon Prime less than forty-eight hours ago. Yet in such a short time, I'd not only met them but given myself to them and reveled in it. I'd held nothing back, for the first time in my life taking what I wanted. Feeling beautiful. Desired. Feminine. Worthy.

This thing with Nik and Sam was supposed to be a fling. A wild time. Fun. They'd changed that when they'd offered me the mating collar, when I'd *felt* their emotions, their desire, their possessive need to protect me. Fuck me. Please me. They'd ruined me, and now I didn't want anyone else. I wanted *them*. They were mine.

"Wait!" I touched my finger to the collar around my neck. The one I'd accepted the night before. "I'd know if they were dead. I'd *feel* it."

Both Jessica and Ander shook their heads, but it was Jessica who spoke. "Oh, honey. No. It's not like that." She touched her own red collar. "They're not Hunters. The collars don't work that far apart. I didn't sense Ander was in danger or share the feelings he had when the Hive attacked. The battlegroup was too far away. I only knew of it when he arrived back at transport. I dropped my breakfast plate, the feelings hit me so hard. I ran out of the palace, my guards chasing after me to get to him at the transport station."

I didn't *feel* either Nik or Sam. Not positively or negatively. I didn't sense them at all. The things I'd felt through the collar weren't bombarding me now. Eagerness, need, pleasure, satisfaction, desire, happiness... all of it had been overwhelming the night before. Sitting here, it was as if the collar was a simple necklace, something pretty about my neck.

Something black. Something that would never change to blue.

"They didn't claim me," I admitted.

"I know, honey." Jessica stroked my back.

Of course she knew. Everyone knew because my collar was black. Would always be black.

"I canceled the royal ball tonight, Lucy. Everyone is on edge. The Hive haven't attacked that deep in Coalition space for months. The kings and queen of Viken have returned to their planet. Commander Karter and the others from Battlegroup Karter have returned to their ship to help with anything they can. Other Prillon fighters have been assigned new missions and transported out. Those from The Colony are waiting to take you back home. I got in touch with Olivia on Earth. She's going to come back from there to be with you."

"Right now?"

"Yes. They are already at the transport pad."

I nodded and moved quickly, throwing the few things I'd brought with me into a bag. I wanted to keep everything I had. I wanted to remember them. Their touch. The sounds they made when they found my body wet and eager for them. Their heat wrapped around me as I slept.

Home. Why did the idea of returning to my tiny quarters on the barren planet feel so empty? Why did I feel so empty? I hadn't been ready to be claimed. I'd told Nik and Sam that. They'd told me how they felt about me, that they'd wanted forever. I'd felt the truth of it in the collar.

That hurt so fucking bad. The potential for what we could have been had been blown up. Destroyed by the Hive.

When I was ready, Jessica led me out of my pretty room. I felt Ander's presence behind us. "Nial's busy in a meeting with the war council... but wanted to be here to talk to you."

"I understand." Her other mate was the head of all of Prillon Prime and the Coalition planets. He had a big job, and losing Ambassador Niklas Lorvar, Sambor and a ship with who knew how many other fighters on it to an unexpected Hive attack was a problem. I didn't have any problems. I was just a makeup artist who was now going to live on The Colony alone. Most likely forever since none of the guys there interested me. Not like Nik and Sam. Now that I knew a true connection, I didn't want anything less.

We met Lindsey, Kiel, Mikki and the others from The Colony at the transport room where the weekend had begun. Everyone was quiet, showing none of the earlier excitement. I got hugs from the ladies, and Lindsey wrapped her arm around me. Two days ago we'd been eager to party and have a fun time on Prillon Prime. I was supposed to get laid.

I'd gotten exactly what I'd come for. Hadn't left with

anything more except... a broken heart. I was devastated. Two smart, brave and amazing guys were dead. I loved them, despite the fact that I was realizing it a little too late.

I looked up at Lindsey. "What happens in Vegas," I said, then burst into tears.

11

Niklas, Uncharted Asteroid, Four Days Later

WE CROUCHED behind a ridge of black carbonite boulders on the asteroid and watched as the Hive Scouts swarmed what remained of our wrecked cargo ship. This was the third scout team in the last few hours. There were four who'd survived the crash. Four of us stuck on this Coalition-forgotten rock. Me, Sambor, Warlord Bahre and Captain Var, a Prillon who'd been outside the meeting room when the explosion had occurred. Either the rest of the passengers on the cargo ship had transported out or had been sucked into space. After days on this hellish planet, I had to wonder if instant death would have been a better option. Now we spent our time avoiding the Hive, staying alive and waiting for rescue.

Lying flat on the rock above us, Sambor had his ion rifle aimed in the Hives' direction. He was practically motionless, watching. His whisper was loud and clear in my helmet.

"Three Scouts. Three Soldiers with heavy armor."

"Fuck." The Atlan's groan fit my own mood perfectly, but the sound was because he was seriously injured. His body was riddled with a patchwork of burns and lacerations that no mere mortal creature should have survived. We'd found one ReGen wand in the wreckage after the crash and it had worked for a time, but without being recharged, it had become as useless as one of the pebbles we lay upon. The Atlan now survived on pure will.

Var crouched on the opposite side of the small plateau we'd climbed after the crash. His ion rifle pointed in the opposite direction, guarding our flank. Above us, a rock overhang created the illusion of a cave. It wasn't much, but the outcropping had protected us from the harsh rays of the nearby star as well as kept us hidden from Hive patrol ships. So far.

The asteroid's electromagnetic field was wreaking havoc with our comms. We could speak to one another, but the connection was weak and filled with interference. And our transport beacons? We had tried, but they had been unable to lock onto a transport location. We were stranded with no way to communicate with the Coalition, and no way off this rock.

Unless help arrived soon, we were all dead. Or worse. If the *worse* happened, we all knew it would be so bad that being sucked into space would have been a blessing.

Why had I thought my job was so important? Why did I risk what we had with Lucy for Helion? The Hive weren't going anywhere. That was blatantly obvious to all of us in this moment. I should have told Helion no. Delayed the meeting. Stayed with Lucy. Duty had called me away.

Look where that got me. All of us.

Fuck.

Sambor remained still for long minutes, and we remained in silence, waiting with him. There was nothing else to do except think about all my own weaknesses. He was the expert here, a veteran of many Hive battles. He knew what he was doing, knew how to keep us alive. If I had to crash-land on a Hive-infested asteroid and remain alive with anyone, it would be him.

"They're inside," Sambor murmured. "I'm coming down. Don't shoot me."

"Not even for fun?" I asked, making Bahre as well as Var chuckle.

Sambor slid down the rocks to land opposite me. I sat next to Bahre, monitoring the status of his life support on his armor's display. There wasn't anything I could do, but it made me feel better knowing his vitals were holding steady. Sambor stretched his legs out and settled his ion rifle across his thighs. "Captain Var, get over here. We need to talk."

The Prillon warrior moved silent as a ghost and completed a triangle in the small area where Sambor was one corner, Bahre and myself the third. He squatted down. "What's the plan?"

"What plan?" I asked. There was no plan. This wasn't a diplomatic trip with meetings and dinners scheduled. This also wasn't a mission, the details having been coordinated in advance.

Sambor looked at me, and the lack of humor in his eyes was startling. "We have waited three days for a ReCon team. They're not coming. Based on the blast and the wreckage, I'm guessing the Coalition already thinks we're dead."

I wanted to argue, to verbalize some kind of hope, especially for Bahre, but I knew Sambor was probably right. "What do we do?" I was used to being in charge. But here? Now? I could fire an ion blaster or take on an enemy in hand-to-hand combat. I could argue or cajole or compliment. I was a master at reading people and figuring out what they wanted. I was a diplomat, not a survivalist. I'd graduated from the Coalition academy along with the rest of them, but our paths had diverged since. Yet we were back together again now. I had to hope Fate had brought the four of us together to get us out of here.

"You are going to stay here with Bahre," Sambor ordered. This wasn't my element, but it was his. "Var and I are going to set up an ambush and steal one of the Hive ships. Then we're going to fly it back into Coalition space and pray for a miracle. Or that we won't be blown out of the sky, again, but this time by our own fighters."

I grimaced at the terrible plan. "We can't fly a Hive ship. We won't even be able to start the damn thing. They'll have it locked down, and we don't have their access codes."

Var stood from his crouch, looming over us. "I can fly it."

That stopped me cold. "How? You're a fine pilot, but

how are you going to get past the Hive security protocols?"

Var tapped the side of his head like that was an answer. When I stared, waiting, he shrugged. "Ask Helion. I can fly it. Trust me."

I looked from Var to Sambor. Obviously being a diplomat didn't mean I knew all the secrets. "You know about this?"

"Yes."

His response made me numb. I knew Helion kept things confidential, but having a Coalition fighter able to hack the Hive security protocols and take over one of their ships? That was something I should have been told.

"Get me down there. I can help." Bahre clenched both of his hands into fists as if summoning his beast for one last hurrah before dying.

"No. You're not going anywhere." I wasn't in charge here, but it was clear Bahre could be of no help. That only made his injuries worse since he knew they hindered him and potentially put all of us in danger. He was a weak link, but I sure as fuck wasn't leaving him behind. I had no doubt Sambor and Var thought the same. My gaze locked with Sambor's. "I can help."

Sambor climbed to his feet and handed me his long-range ion rifle. "You aren't going anywhere near those Hive. But you can shoot."

"Indeed."

"The Hive have been cycling through every sixty-three minutes."

"What?"

"Exactly every sixty-three minutes," Var confirmed.

Sambor sorted his gear as the Prillon watched. He, apparently, was ready to go. Sambor checked the power setting on his ion blaster, a second blaster, a blade designed to cut through armor, and his air supply. We only had a few hours left before our suits ran dry. We hadn't eaten anything in over a day. It was now or never.

When he was satisfied, he looked at me, then Bahre.

"I'm going down to the wreckage, lure them out and away from their ship. I'm going to come at them from the rock formation at the rear of the craft. Niklas, you wait until I give you the signal, then take down as many as you can from up here."

"What about me?" Var asked.

Sambor's focused gaze shifted. "You are going to locate the nearest ship and steal it. Then you're going to get it up here, load up Niklas and Bahre."

"And you?" I asked.

"If it's clear, I'll signal you to drop down and open the hatch. If not, you get the fuck off this rock and don't look back. I'll kill as many as I can."

Fuck. No. "No, Sam."

I purposely used Lucy's nickname for him to remind him that he had to get off this rock as well. We had a mate to take care of. A life to live. Dying on this stupid asteroid was not part of the plan. "I'm not leaving you here. It's my fault we're here. My duty put us in danger."

Sambor's rage rushed through the collar until I nearly choked on the strength of his feelings.

Rage. Anguish. Determination. No fear. There was no fear.

"And it's my duty that will get us out. Later you can

evaluate your priorities." He leaned in close, our helmets nearly touching. "You listen to me. We're here because of the Hive. Sure, maybe you need to consider taking some days off, but you're seeing what's important now. Lucy. And she needs one of us to survive. You are her mate. You claimed her. You put the Lorvar collar around her neck and named me your second. You will survive. You will take care of her. That is your job, your duty. You will get off this rock."

"And what of you, Sam? You are not going to sacrifice yourself to save me. I won't allow it."

"If we pull this off, we'll all be going home. But if you need to leave to ensure Bahre gets to care and Var gets his ass out of here for another mission, you will." Sambor checked the ion rifle and held it out to me. He pointed up. "There. Right where I was. Maybe three paces to the left. That should give you the best view of the wreckage. Don't shoot until I give you the signal." Sambor held out the rifle until I took it, but I wasn't done with this fight.

"What about Lucy? You will break her heart. She can't lose you."

Sambor ignored me, began to walk away, Var on his heels. I tried to stand, but Bahre's huge hand settled in the center of my chest and shoved me back to the ground. "Let him go."

"I can't." He was Lucy's second, my lifelong friend. I was not worthy of this sacrifice.

"You can and you must," he replied through gritted teeth. "Is this not the very reason you Prillons choose a second? So that one of you always remains to take care of your female?"

I didn't respond. It was not an actual question. The Atlan already knew the answer. I watched Sambor and Var walk away and disappear around one of the black rock outcroppings I knew would provide a place they could safely scramble down into the crevasse where our ship had crashed. Where they would set up an ambush for at least six Hive, maybe more.

I leaned back against the rock and stared up at the twinkling stars spread overhead like billions of sparkling jewels. Space was the ultimate in opposites. Extreme beauty with extreme danger. The time we'd spent on this asteroid was a prime example. "We haven't claimed her yet."

"But she's yours." Bahre grunted in pain, the first sign of weakness he'd given, and my heart jumped with concern. We had to get off this asteroid. No one was coming. No one knew we were here.

"She's mine. Mine and Sambor's."

"Is your second capable of defeating six Hive alone?"

I considered the question. "Yes. He is." The words were not a lie. Sambor had been trained in the Coalition's special forces program. He'd fought the Hive for years before settling into what he considered a life of luxury, guarding me. He'd done it because I'd asked, and because the IC had begun sending me into more and more dangerous situations. Prime Nial had demanded someone go meet with the legions on Rogue 5, scout out Sector Zero and the other lawless regions technically within Coalition space. He'd sent me. I'd taken Sambor with me. "He's saved my life more than once."

"Then let him do his job and go home. His strategy is

sound, and you know it. Take care of your female. Do you wish her to lose both of you?"

That made the blood run cold as ice in my veins. I could not allow Lucy to feel such loss. Such pain. "No. That is unacceptable."

Bahre grunted. "That's what I thought. Get your head on straight, Prillon. Fight like an Atlan, like a fucking beast to get back to her."

"I am no beast." I was a fucking Prillon warrior with a mate and my second to protect. I would do what Sambor ordered. He would trust me to be in position, to cover him. I would not let him down.

Cold and calm, I climbed to the top of the boulder Sambor had indicated that would give me the tactical advantage. I waited patiently as the minutes passed, thinking of nothing but killing. Surviving. Making sure Sambor and I both returned to our mate.

Lucy deserved no less than what I had promised her. All of me. Every cell and fiber and ounce of will was hers. I would fight until my dying breath to get back to her... and to take Sambor with me.

He wasn't going to have to kill very many Hive. I was going to wreak havoc on those fuckers from here. Every. Last. One.

Bright light appeared overhead, and I watched as three Hive ships landed within easy walking distance of our ship's wreckage, most likely sensing Sambor's presence. Hidden in the rocks nearby, he remained still as the stone around him, his armor shifting color to match the black rocks at his back. He was nothing more than a shadow.

I could not see Var at all but knew he would be nearby, watching the Hive land, deciding which ship to take.

As expected, three Hive exited each ship and walked toward the wreckage. One was a trio of very large and heavily armed Hive Soldiers, most likely captured and integrated Prillon warriors. The second group of three were Hive Scouts. Small, fast and aggressive. They looked as if they could have once been human, Viken or even Everian fighters. Then there was the last group. One of them was taller than anyone I'd ever seen—and that included Atlans in beast mode. He was dark blue and was not wearing armor. His face looked like his skin had been put together in pieces sewn with silver thread, and his entire body was a patchwork of different shades of blue.

I'd seen this kind of pattern before in just one creature—the Nexus unit Helion kept locked up at Core Command. This one looked almost exactly like that Nexus unit that had been imprisoned on our ship before we crashed, the blue fucker that Helion had been so desperate to crack that he'd arranged the meeting in deep space with Gwen.

But this Nexus unit was not the same male as the prisoner. This one's silver streak bisecting his face was in a diagonal slash from forehead to ear, not vertical, as Helion's captive's was.

What the fuck was a Nexus unit doing on this worthless asteroid? Inspecting our ship?

Then Makarios's words returned to me. *They fucking track her like Elite Everian Hunters.*

The Nexus unit and his team were hunting Gwen,

thinking she was here, looking for clues. My breath caught. Rage filled me at the desperation they had to track her. No wonder Gwen and Mak were so uncomfortable and cagey about meeting.

The blue Nexus unit was taller than the Scouts and Soldiers by at least two feet. Large, black bulbous additions ran along the base of his skull and connected to his spine like fingers digging into the flesh of his back. He walked freely, no armor necessary, despite the lack of atmosphere and freezing temperature on the surface of the asteroid. I watched him through my rifle's scope and shuddered at the pure, lifeless black of his eyes. Walking with him were two more Hive the likes of which I had never seen before. They were huge—not as big as the Nexus unit himself, but larger than the others. Thicker. Taller.

Fuck. Those two were Atlans. Or they used to be. The three moved together, the Nexus unit in the center and the integrated Atlan Hive bodyguards on either side of him for protection. The other six Hive, the Soldiers and Scouts, fanned out along the ground surrounding the wreckage, picking up debris and running scans.

We were fucked. Nine Hive in total. We might have been able to take them out, but not with two integrated Atlan Hive who were beast sized and a Nexus unit. I didn't say a word, not wanting our comms to alert them to our presence, but I wanted to shout at Sambor to get the fuck out of there and wait—wait for a different batch of Hive to arrive—one without a Nexus unit. Without integrated Atlan Warlords.

Just... wait.

But we had no choice. We were all running low on air, and our suits would last one more day at the most.

What if the Nexus unit left and no Hive ever came back? What if there was not another chance to steal a ship?

We had to fight. An Atlan in full armor was nearly impossible to take down with standard weapons on a good day. These were integrated Atlans who appeared to be permanently frozen in beast mode.

I would have to aim for the head... and not miss.

Fuck.

How did the Nexus unit control the integrated Atlans? And not just one, but two?

There was nothing I could do now. Sambor had, no doubt, seen them as well. Even if I risked warning him about the integrated Altan Hive, I knew my warning would fall on deaf ears. He was doing this, one way or another, no matter the odds. No, he was doing what his training dictated, what he'd been taught, practiced in battle. He was doing his job, despite the odds. If I argued with him, I was being insubordinate, and stupid. Deep down I knew he was correct in his plan. He was determined to get me—all of us—off this planet alive, and I had to respect his command. His honor. Doing anything else would not only undermine his command but show disrespect to my second. I would not dishonor him in such a manner.

Sambor waited until the Nexus unit entered the hull of the wreckage and disappeared from view, taking one fully integrated Atlan bodyguard with him. The other beast stood at the entrance as if guarding the Nexus from his own Hive Scouts and Soldiers.

Interesting.

With a bellow worthy of any Atlan, Sambor leaped from hiding and opened fire, taking down two Scouts closest to him before dashing behind a boulder.

The three heavier Hive Soldiers moved as one to surround him. I could have finished one of them out, but I waited. Sambor had not given me his signal. Stubborn bastard.

Breathing slowly, keeping calm, I kept my rifle aimed at the entrance to the wreckage, hoping the Nexus unit would show himself.

Seconds later he did.

"Now!" Sambor screamed the command, and I pulled the trigger.

The Nexus unit took the hit to his chest and staggered back but did not fall. I fired again. Again.

The integrated Atlan Hive with him bellowed with rage and raced after the Nexus unit, who was moving like... fucking incredible. I'd never seen anything move that fast, especially after being shot with an ion rifle. Not even an Elite Everian Hunter.

He was coming for me, following the trajectory of the ion strike.

I fired again, but the shot seemed to bounce off the Nexus unit as if I were throwing pebbles, not hitting him with one of our strongest weapons, even as he moved closer.

Scrambling back, I made my way to Bahre and helped him to his feet. "We have to move. Now!"

Bahre stumbled for a moment, then righted himself. "What is happening?"

"Sambor is taking on three Soldiers and a Scout. He got two of them." I tugged at him to force him to move toward the far edge of the small outcropping where I could take cover on a slight overhang and try to kill the Nexus up close and personal. "We have a Nexus unit and two integrated Atlan Hive in beast mode coming at us faster than I've ever seen anything move."

His pained gaze met mine. "Two Atlans?"

I nodded. "Yes. And they can't keep up with the Nexus unit. Move!"

Bahre leaned on my shoulder as we moved toward the rocks I knew would be the best place to make our last stand. Bahre leaned against the rock, his bulk partially hidden behind me as I positioned myself and my ion rifle to shoot the moment the Nexus unit cleared the boulders in front of us.

Seconds later the Nexus unit appeared like a wild animal chasing prey.

I fired. Direct hit to his abdomen.

Nothing. It didn't even slow the fucker down.

He stood in front of me and yanked the rifle from my hands, then snapped it in half like it was a twig. "Where is my female?" His voice was deep and mechanical, and there was not an ounce of emotion or battle rage in the question. *His female?*

"I don't know what you're talking about." I thought to stall him with my response as I motioned Bahre with my hand to move. Get the fuck out of here.

Run.

"My mate," he added. "Her name is Gwendolyn. She was here, on your ship. Where is she now?"

This was more words than the Nexus unit Helion had been interrogating had spoken in the months we'd had him captive. I avoided looking the blue monster in the eye, but it was hard. The pull to do so was strong. I remembered those dark, lifeless orbs would suck me in and drown me. I'd learned that the hard way, staring at our captive the first time Helion had taken me to see him. Sambor had saved me, knocking me to the side, breaking the Nexus unit's hold on my mind.

Wiser now, I stared at this one's chest, not daring to glance up, not for a moment. Once he had control of my mind, I'd tell him anything he wanted to know. And I knew a lot.

I'd fought the Hive my entire career but had never been face-to-face with one. Never fought one. Up close, this one was... blue. Focused. Not real. The metal integrations gleamed in the starlight, reminding me this thing was not... one of us. It moved and spoke and killed, but it did not *live*.

Behind him, the two integrated Atlans appeared, clawing and climbing their way to stand where Bahre and I had been just a few moments ago. Bahre hadn't moved. Damn him.

"Get the fuck out of here, Bahre. Sam. Take their ship and go." Silence was no longer important, and one of us had to live. "Get back to Lucy." Reaching behind me, I wrapped my palm around the handle of a blade I kept on my hip for emergencies.

"Who is Lucy?" the Nexus unit asked.

"None of your fucking business." I wanted to scream at this thing but knew it would be futile.

In my peripheral vision, I watched the Nexus unit tilt his head to the side as if curious. "I sense no fear. Good. You will be one of us now."

I swiped up with my dagger, aiming for what I hoped would be the Nexus unit's heart. Or central processing unit. Something... critical. The Nexus unit looked down to where my blade was buried in his chest and pulled it out slowly, the metal coated in thick, black liquid that looked more like tar than blood. "You resist." He tossed the blade aside and reached for me.

"No!" Bahre bellowed and stepped forward, moving fast, faster than he should have been capable of with his injuries. He was in full beast mode, his body huge, his rage like a volcanic eruption. "No, Atlans!"

The Nexus unit looked up in shock, and I realized he'd been so fixated on me that he hadn't seen Bahre hiding behind me. Ah, the Hive did have emotions, of sorts. It had not calculated that I had company.

Bahre took the Nexus by the neck, lifted him from the ground and... pulled his head off his body with a sickening slurping sound. Black tar blood spewed from the neck of the creature, spraying Bahre's armor and helmet, covering his shoulders and chest.

Behind the Nexus, the two Atlans fell to the ground as if suddenly released from a trance, screaming inside their helmets, their agony making Bahre's beast roar in response. In challenge? I didn't understand what was happening, but even inside my helmet, the sound made my head ring.

"What the fuck is going on up there?" Sambor's voice was crystal clear and calm. Shockingly calm.

"Bahre just ripped the head off a Nexus unit. The two integrated Atlans with him are responding. They're free of Hive control."

"That would explain it." Var's relief was clear in his own voice. "I've got a ship. There were three more Scouts inside. They just dropped dead."

"Same here," Sambor replied. "I had one more Soldier to take down. An integrated Prillon. He just hit his knees. If he survives, we'll have to take him with us."

I stood and pulled the ion pistol from my holster. The ion rifle was toast, and this little blaster would probably just make the Atlans writhing in pain on the ground angry—but it was all I had. "The two integrated Atlans are up here on the ground. They are no longer a threat."

"Do not hurt them." Bahre was still in beast mode, but there was so much blood inside his helmet I had no idea how he was standing, let alone talking.

"I won't shoot them as long as they don't try to kill us."

That made Bahre snort. He grabbed the small ion blaster from my hand and tossed it aside like it was an old shoe. "Not hurt. Rage. Relief."

"Yes, I figured that."

Bahre went to stand over the two fallen, integrated Warlords and let out a battle cry I had never heard before.

In my headset, Sambor chuckled. "Gods be damned, that is music to my ears."

"What the fuck is that?"

"Warlord victory cry. You should hear a battalion of Atlans after they rip apart a battlefield full of Hive."

The bright light of a ship caught my attention as it settled on the ground below us. I watched as a hatch opened and Sambor climbed on board, hauling the injured Prillon Hive Soldier with him. Moments later the ship hovered above us, ramp down, Sambor on the other end with his hand out.

Bahre handed first one, then the second Atlan up to Sambor, who reached out and took them on board without question.

"Grab that Nexus head," Var told me. "Helion will want it."

Disgusted but knowing Var was correct, I picked up the blue head—tentacles and gadgets attached—and threw it up to Sambor.

"Forget that. He'll want the body, too."

"Gods be damned. Why are we catering to that asshole?" I looked back to where the massive corpse lay unmoving, knew this was an opportunity my dislike for the commander shouldn't prevent. "Go, Bahre." I used my shoulder to help Bahre get to Sambor, then went back for the body.

It took every ounce of strength I possessed to move the thing a few feet. Bahre appeared next to me. "Move."

I glanced up in shock. "You can barely walk, Warlord. I'll handle this."

His beast was calming, and Bahre was able to speak in a full sentence. "You are stubborn. I do not know how you got a female to accept you." He picked up the Nexus corpse with a grunt and walked up the ramp. Sambor clapped him on the back, which made the injured Warlord drop the body with another grunt of pain.

I actually laughed at his insult, a sound I hadn't been sure I would ever hear again. Our fight had been intense, only perhaps five or ten minutes, but it was clear now that we would survive.

With all four of us who'd made it through the crash—and a few new additions—safely climbing on board, Sambor walked down the ramp and the two of us managed to drag the dead body onto the stolen Hive ship.

"Fucker is heavy. Too heavy." It was like the Nexus unit was made of magnets that literally locked it to the gravitational field beneath it. He was far heavier than his size should have dictated, even if he were made of pure stone or metal.

"Helion can have fun dissecting him."

I grunted at that. Without doubt, Sambor was right.

He held out his hand to me. "Get on, Nik. Lucy will be worried. Let's go home and claim her."

Home. Fuck. I liked the sound of that.

ucy, Interior Child's Play Area, The Colony

I SAT in one of the beanbag chairs and watched the kids play, tuning out their chatter and laughter. With the number of kids growing on the planet pretty darn fast, a playroom had been built where the kids could burn off energy. The space had pint-size tables and chairs for crafts, a large rug for story time, a reading corner with picture and word books, and a fast-food-chain type playland. The guys had seen pictures we'd shared of these Earth indoor playgrounds and added their own planets' spin. Slides and tubes, ropes and ladders, poles and rock walls. It was a little nuts, especially since the bulk of the kids were under the age of two. But they'd grow into it— and based on the size of the Prillons, but especially the Atlans, really fast. I wished I were a little shorter so I could join them in the corner where there was a fake tree to be reached from a small spaceship by a bridge.

Emma had dragged me over to the beanbag in the reading nook and pointed her little finger for me to sit. She kept watch to make sure I remained. She was a bossy thing, and it was amusing to observe the toddler imitate Wulf. Olivia dragged a tiny chair over to sit beside me. She and Wulf had returned from Earth the day before, earlier than expected since Rachel had commed her about what had happened. I had a feeling they were pleased to leave Earth behind.

I had no idea if they'd wrapped up their PR work for the *Bachelor Beast*, and I didn't really care. I'd enjoyed working on the show and approved of the idea behind the concept—bringing attention to worthy fighters who wanted mates—but didn't miss Chet or the pettiness that came with reality TV. There was none of that here in space. I'd only been behind the camera. As for Olivia and Wulf, who'd had every aspect of their relationship broadcast all over the world, they probably didn't care either. As soon as a new bachelor beast was assigned, the spotlight would be off them and on to the new Atlan.

I had no interest in anything, feeling numb and strangely surreal. If I didn't have the black collar about my neck, I'd have questioned my sanity and wondered if the two days on Prillon Prime had actually happened.

I had no pictures, no selfies or visual record of Nik and Sam. I'd gone onto the computer and searched for them, found their images and bios, which proved they did exist.

Had.

They were dead.

Dead.

I could still remember their touch. Their weight as they pressed me into the bed. Their breath. Their voices. The heft of their cocks as they filled me.

A shriek of laughter broke through my dirty thoughts. Tanner and Wyatt wore kid-sized Coalition uniforms, armor and all, and ran around with toy ion pistols making weird blaster sounds. They were fighting imaginary Hive and hiding behind the toddler slide, their heads popping out to shoot. Emma was currently in the ball pit tossing the colored orbs up in the air.

Olivia and I were the only adults in the room. When I glanced at the clock on the wall, I saw that Lindsey would come to take over supervision in twenty minutes. There was an unspoken arrangement that we'd watch the kids in shifts to give everyone a little break. This way the kids could keep playing but the parents could rest.

"Ready to talk about it?" Olivia asked.

I glanced up at her. Even in the kiddie chair, she was taller than me. I sighed. "I have to, since you forced me out of bed."

After transporting back with the others, I'd gone right to my quarters and climbed into bed. And stayed. Food had been dropped off, even though I had an S-Gen machine, but I'd been left alone.

Until Olivia came storming into my room, then ripped the covers off the bed and made me shower and put on fresh clothes.

"You were starting to smell," she replied, although

there was no scolding in her tone. "Just tell me about the party. I missed everything."

Now she grumbled.

"Jessica wanted to line dance, so a DJ—or some guy with a sound system Lindsey must have either imported from Earth or magically programmed an S-Gen machine to make—" I took a breath. "They played the Electric Slide."

Olivia's eyes widened; then she burst out laughing. "Oh God, I can only imagine."

I couldn't help but crack a smile. "Those big, buff, in-control aliens?"

She put her fingers over her lips to hide her grin. "Can't dance?"

I shook my head. "Can't dance. Everyone was bumping into each other. Except this one Prillon commander. Now *he* had moves."

Emma tossed a soft ball up in the air, and it bounced off her head.

"Wulf would have stepped on me," Olivia said.

"Nik ran into me. That's how we met." A pang of longing filled me at the memory of us bumping, of him grabbing me so I didn't fall. Ensuring I wasn't hurt.

"Was he a fair Prillon or dark? I heard they're like various colors of caramel."

"Nik was dark, Sam fair."

"One of each. Mmm." Her eyes widened. "Were they good?" she asked, glancing at the kids. "Tanner, be careful running near Emma."

Tanner fired his weapon, and a light on Wyatt's armor turned green.

"I'm not the Hive!" Wyatt shouted, mad he'd been hit.

Olivia had to go over and talk to the boys, and I took a moment to think. Were Nik and Sam good?

So good. My pussy clenched. I ran my fingers over the smooth collar.

Olivia returned, saw the gesture. She dropped into the chair, her knees bent up by her shoulders.

"Are you going to take that off?"

I shrugged. "It was supposed to be a fling. I just wanted to get laid. I made it clear. Really, really clear."

She rolled her eyes. "You remember how Wulf literally moved in even though I told him we wouldn't work."

I'd been there when Wulf arrived at Olivia's house, staked his claim. I should have realized from his actions how Nik and Sam would behave. The difference was, Wulf was Atlan and in mating fever at the time. He'd taken one look at Olivia on the *Bachelor Beast* set and *known.*

"They didn't come on to me. I propositioned them," I clarified.

Olivia grinned. "You go, girl."

I glanced away, suddenly feeling sad. Or sadder.

"You don't think they'd have dragged you out of there if you hadn't made the first move? You know Prillons. They're just as bossy as Atlans."

I pursed my lips. "True."

She was quiet for a minute, waved to Emma. "But it was more than a fling for them. You're wearing a collar."

"I refused to be claimed. I didn't... I didn't—"

She set her hand on my shoulder as I swallowed tears that were lodged in my throat.

"I didn't believe them," I whispered.

"Don't the collars share their feelings?"

I nodded.

"It's not like they could lie. It's not like on Earth when you don't know if a guy's just lying for sex."

I shifted in the beanbag, bringing my knee up so I could face her. "I knew. I felt the truth. They showed it to me. Then they left for their meeting and... well, there wasn't time."

She squeezed my shoulder. "And now?"

I touched the collar again.

"Now I'm alone here." I sighed. "I'm sorry. I don't mean that you and Wulf and the kids aren't my family and I'm not *alone*. But... I know what having mates is like. I almost had my own family, and now I want it. Want what you and Wulf have. What Nik and Sam offered."

Olivia was quiet as she studied me. "Yeah, it's not the same thing."

"I came here to be with you guys. I don't regret it, but now I know what I'm missing. You have a life with Wulf. I don't have anything here. I'm just the fifth wheel."

"I know it's too soon, but you could mate someone else."

I didn't want anyone else, but I couldn't tell Olivia that. Instead I rolled my eyes and tried for some levity. "That would only work if Wulf lays off his big-brother thing."

As if he knew we were talking about him, the playroom door slid open and he came in, his head almost grazing the top. "Who's hunting Hive?" His voice boomed through the room, and Tanner and Wyatt froze, spun in place and raised their hands.

Wulf went over and dropped to his knees so he was closer to their height. "Did you look behind the ship?"

They nodded, their heads bobbing in unison.

"We should check again because Hive are known to be tricky and devious. Climb on, fighters."

Wulf dropped to his hands, and Tanner and Wyatt climbed on as if riding a horse. Wulf crawled toward the back of the room. "Weapons ready!"

"Braun's interested," Olivia said, smiling at her mate's antics. He was a good father, a good role model for the boys. Emma chased after them, tugging on Wulf's arm until he grinned and lifted her up to sit on the back of his neck where she squealed, pointed and screamed, "Go!"

"Wulf threatened to beat him bloody in the pit if he even breathed near me," I reminded.

"He still talked with you... when Wulf wasn't around." She rubbed her arms as if the topic made her as uncomfortable as it was making me. "He would worship you. You know he would. You may not be *the one* for each other, but you could be happy."

I sighed. "Braun's sweet, Liv. You know that. He's a nice guy, but I'm not for him. God, he's like a big brother. I know it, and I think he knows it, too. That Atlan is a looker, and I'm sure he'll claim some female in that hot up-against-the-wall sort of way. It just won't be me."

Olivia fanned herself, probably remembering the time Wulf carried her out of the *Bachelor Beast* studio... on live TV.

"I think Braun feels stuck, like me," I admitted.

"You're not stuck. You've got big plans."

Shaking my head, I looked at my lap. "I did everyone's hair and makeup for the party. It was so much fun. Sure, I cut hair for Rachel, you and the others, but there's less than ten women on the planet. I can't run a spa for ten women."

Olivia laughed, tugged on one of my curls. "I'd come every day."

I rolled my eyes, thought of Sam and how he'd found my hair... wild. "Whatever. No women, no spa."

She scrunched up her face, then smiled when Emma came running over. She climbed into Olivia's lap as the boys continued to play with Wulf.

"Think you want to go back to Earth, then? You're the only one of us who has that choice."

That was a good question. Did I? Unlike Olivia, I was able to go back. I could start up a spa like I wanted. I knew how it should be done. How to get a business license and a loan and everything. There, I could do it. But after being in space, I wasn't sure if it was for me.

"I'm different, Liv. Two nights with two guys and I had everything. I'd say yes to being claimed. I was willing to leave here, leave *you* for two hot studs."

"For two hot studs, I'd leave me, too."

I sighed, her joke falling flat. "I'm serious. I'd say yes to them. To all of it."

Olivia's eyes widened at my vehemence.

"Now it's not going to happen." I pushed myself out of the beanbag chair, looked down at Olivia with Emma, who was sucking her thumb. "I'm going back to bed. I'm okay. I just need time."

I felt like I had tons of it. I had no real job, no real prospects. No Nik and Sam. Braun was going to be a problem because I had a feeling his mating fever was pushing him toward me. I just didn't want to break his heart, because I knew exactly what walking around with a broken heart felt like.

Empty.

13

*S*ambor, The Colony

I'D NEVER BEEN to The Colony before. Niklas had said he'd been once, but that had been before I'd become his guard. Seeing the barren landscape through the windows, it reminded me of the planet we'd just escaped. Except here, there were no Hive—I hoped—and we'd arrived intentionally. Crash-landing was something I wanted to experience only once.

Governor Maxim had met us in the transport room. Alone.

Disappointment coursed through me at not having Lucy waiting for us. We'd flown the fucking Hive craft into Coalition-controlled space, and all four of us initiated our comms to let them know we were friendly. The last thing we'd wanted to do was be shot out of the sky a second time. We'd had the medical station connect with

Bahre's comm so they could transport him directly to the unit for emergency medical treatment. At the time we'd had no idea of his chances for survival. He'd been without care for four days, but we'd learned since that time in a ReGen pod had healed his injuries, although he'd be scarred physically for life.

As for the rest of us, we'd flown the Hive ship to Battleship Karter, since it was the closest ship in the sector, and the Hive craft would be kept and studied for technology and enhancements. Helion had met us when we arrived—completely unscathed from the attack—to collect the Nexus unit's two parts, the body and separated head. I'd been so glad to be back on Coalition turf that I hadn't paid him any attention. We'd all gone to medical, been examined and released. The two rescued Atlan Warlords and the Prillon warrior would have their integrations analyzed, but were eventually headed for The Colony and a second chance. Var would spend a few days on the Karter to recuperate before being assigned a new mission. As for Niklas and myself, we'd only taken time to eat, shower and don fresh clothes before going to the transport room to be sent directly to The Colony.

No, not to The Colony. To Lucy. Our mate.

In the blink of an eye, we arrived, eagerly going down the steps to the governor. He slapped me on the shoulder and gave us both a broad smile. "It is good to see you both."

"Governor," Niklas began but was cut off.

"Do not fear, your mate is nearby," Governor Maxim assured us.

I was not as schooled at hiding my emotions like Niklas. "Where is she? Why is she not here?"

"She does not know of your arrival." He frowned for a moment. "Or that you're alive."

"That is cruel," Niklas replied.

"I assure you, it was far from that. I heard of your survival and that of the others. And the rescue of a few who will make The Colony their new home. As for Lucy, I didn't wish to falsely inflate any hopes she might have if the comms I'd received were wrong or if, hell, you somehow got sucked out a waste chute."

I stared at the governor with wide eyes. Waste chute?

He sighed. "Never mind."

Niklas inspected Governor Maxim like he'd lost his mind. "You were afraid we would not come for her."

Maxim sighed. "I could not risk breaking her heart again. She has been... struggling... since the news of the explosion."

"I placed my collar around her neck, Governor. She is mine. I demand to see her. Now." The idea of her suffering was causing Niklas immense pain. My reaction was more along the lines of rage that this Prillon ass would dare deny our mate the comfort we could provide, and disgust at his lack of faith in fellow warriors.

"Lucy is ours. We will fight every fucking integrated bastard on this planet if you try to keep her from us." I meant every word. The potent effect of Niklas's pain mixed with my rage and disgust was making us both a bit... unstable. We needed our mate.

Apparently *that* was the kind of reaction Governor Maxim Rone appreciated and understood. With a chuckle, he put his hands up in surrender and turned to the transport tech. "Where is Lucy Vandermark?"

The tech ran his fingers over the controls, looked to the governor. "Main cafeteria."

The governor murmured his thanks. "Follow me."

The governor led us down a labyrinth of corridors. He was walking too slowly, but even though I wasn't the diplomat, I knew not to yell at him to move faster. The scent of food hit me before we arrived, and I knew— hoped—this was the right place. That our mate would be behind the door we were approaching.

I glanced at Niklas. I didn't have to see the tense line of his shoulders to know he was as worried as I. The collars shared all his concerns with me. The last time we'd been with Lucy, she'd accepted the collar about her neck, but not our claim. Did she still feel the same way? Had she decided she didn't want the collar any longer? Hell, had she removed it?

It was right then when I realized something, grabbed Niklas's arm. He looked my way. "I don't feel her."

His eyes widened as he paused. "You're right. Governor, has Lucy removed her collar?"

The governor rubbed his chin. "No. It is still black about her neck. You don't feel her emotions?"

We shook our heads.

He tipped his, moved to stand so the doors sensed him and opened. "Then go find out why."

I took a deep breath, resigned to whatever came next. We'd survived four days behind enemy territory. I'd done so with the motivation to get back to Lucy to tell her how I felt, how Niklas and I wanted to claim her. We'd take all the time she needed, but we would not be giving her up. We knew what life was like without her, and that was not a life we wanted to live.

———

Lucy

I TRIED TO EAT. I did. Rachel had even brought me my favorite pizza, fresh from the S-Gen machine.

But everything tasted like ash in my mouth. I was numb. I felt nothing because when I did feel, the only thing inside me was pain. So I buried it. Crushed it under my heel like an insect. Dead.

If I couldn't feel what I had with Sam and Nik wrapped around me, I'd rather not feel anything.

We sat at a large, round table. Rachel and little Max were arguing about which vegetables he was going—or *not* going—to eat. The little boy was adorable, preferring Earth carrots over a bright yellow plant from Prillon Prime, but refusing to eat anything green.

Seemed that even in space, the green veggies came in a hard last.

Normally the thought would have made me smile, but now I felt nothing. I imagined that I was an android, a computer, someone like that character, Data, from *Star Trek*. Except hadn't he *wanted* to be human? To feel emotion?

I was the opposite of late, perfectly content to feel nothing.

The Warlord, Braun, had been watching me with undisguised worry in his eyes. Even now he sat at the table next to Caroline and Rezzer, one twin on each of his knees. They adored him, as all the children did, and his singing voice was like an angel's.

I hadn't even known Atlans could sing until he'd taken a crying Emma a few days after our arrival and sung her to sleep in two minutes flat. That day had been a revelation, and Olivia had badgered Wulf until he relented and the two Warlords sang a loud, rollicking battle song that reminded me of a drunken Irish bar ditty. That day I'd made a friend. Braun *was* dear to me, but he wasn't meant to be mine. And his beast did not demand he take me.

Neither one of us wanted to settle, but we had flirted with possibilities until I met my real mates.

And lost them.

A twinge of pain made me clutch at my stomach, and Rachel glanced at me from under her lashes, her hand moving to rest on top of mine where I'd kept my clenched fist hidden under the table.

I smiled my thanks as Braun listened to the twins' chatter. To them, he was their *Uncle B*. He would make a wonderful mate and father.

Just not mine.

"Aren't you hungry?" Rachel asked. "I can get you something else."

"I'm fine. Thank you. You've done enough. Really." I didn't want pizza. I didn't want anything. I just wanted to go back to my room and stare at the ceiling. Sleep. When

I slept, I dreamed of Niklas and Sambor. In my dreams they were mine again.

Before she could offer to do anything else, I stood. Braun watched me with sad eyes, but we both knew the truth. Any chance we might have had to fall in love had been gone the moment I met my real mates.

"I'm not very hungry. I'm going to go back to my room." I did my best to smile but knew the effort was weak and pathetic. "I'll see everyone tomorrow."

"Okay. Sweet dreams. Comm me if you need anything." Rachel was too kind. She was a good friend. I knew Ryston was on patrol tonight, but where was the governor? He rarely missed spending time with his mate and son.

Turning, I heard his voice in the hallway just before the door to the room slid open.

And I saw ghosts.

Every ounce of raw agony I'd suppressed the last couple of days erupted inside me like a bomb exploding, and my knees collapsed.

Even before I hit the ground, Nik was there, holding me. Sam moved in next to him, and I sobbed, touching them, feeling their faces, their shoulders, their hair. "Are you real?"

"Yes, mate. We are real."

The floodgates opened, and their emotions filled me through the collars. Pain. Relief. Fear for me. Desire. Devotion. Love. God, the jumble scrambled my brain until all I could do was cry and cling to them.

Governor Maxim cleared his throat. "Hey, everyone,

maybe we can all clear out and give these three a little privacy?"

Feet shuffled. I heard one of the twins ask, "Who's that?"

Braun answered. "Those two Prillon warriors are your Aunt Woocy's mates."

"Aunt Woocy has mates?"

I giggled through my tears at little CJ's confusion. I was confused, too.

"Yes, she does." Braun sounded solemn but resigned, and I hoped he found the most amazing woman in the history of the universe to love him. He deserved it.

I lifted my head to watch the last of the crowd shuffle out the doors and saw Governor Maxim slap Braun on the back.

"Don't worry, Warlord. I have big plans for you."

Braun turned his head. "What plans?"

The governor smiled. "You are going to be The Colony's next representative on the *Bachelor Beast* television program on Earth."

Rachel squealed and clapped her hands as the doors slid closed behind them, leaving me alone with my mates.

"Lucy?" Nik's voice was strong, but the fear coming through his collar was going to keep me on my knees.

Rising to a kneeling position, I wrapped one arm around each of my mates and tackled them to the ground. "I love you. I love you both so much."

I gave up trying to hide my emotions and allowed them to flood me—and them. Love. Relief. Gratitude that they were alive. Longing. Need. Pain. I gave them everything. *Everything.*

"Lucy." Sam clutched at my back, ran his hand through my hair, stroked my hip, kissed every part of me he could reach. "Mate, I love you. I need you. Thank the gods."

Nik *clung.* There was no other word for the fierceness of his hold or the rock-solid grip of his hands. He did not move, did not speak, simply held me like he'd never, ever let me go again. And love? God. His absolute devotion poured through the collars like pure heat, pure need.

"You are mine, mate. You are my heart and my soul and my life. Do you understand?"

"Yes." I held on to them both and cried until I didn't have any tears left. Then I cursed. "You let me cry but didn't tell me what happened to you!"

They eyed me, jaws clenched. "It matters not. We are here, and we are not leaving you. Someday we will share what happened. Not now."

It must have been awful, whatever they'd endured. They were right, and I felt their need to not relive it and share it with me but to move on. They were here. I was theirs. "This fucking collar needs to be blue, not black. Blue. You two are mine, understand? Mine. And I want you both to know it."

They didn't argue. Nik stood first. Sam followed and they lifted me to walk between them.

"Once again, mate, are you asking us to accompany you to your private quarters and see to your pleasure?" Nik asked.

I laughed with pure joy. "Yes. That's exactly what I'm asking."

"I do not have a problem with giving you pleasure," Nik said. "Do you, Sambor?"

"Absolutely not."

I realized they were repeating the exact same words they'd said to me at the palace, and my heart melted. These two were mine, and it was time to make it permanent.

 *iklas*

"You make us proud, mate," I said, holding Lucy's hand as Sambor followed, one step behind. She could sense our satisfaction in her through the collars.

A near-death experience filtered out the things that weren't important and added value to those that were. Like Lucy. She was the most crucial thing in the universe.

We'd been given a second chance. Our feelings, the depth of them, couldn't be hidden. Not now. Not when we were all prepared to focus on what really mattered.

All the time stuck on that asteroid, I'd wondered of Lucy's true feelings. She'd made it clear we were just a fling, as humans called it. We were disposable.

No longer. We didn't need the collars to know her heart. The look on her face when she'd first seen us in the canteen told us everything we needed to know.

I saw her love, felt it through the collars, but hearing the true depths of need when she'd said the words aloud filled my heart completely. I'd thought it full before, but there had been something missing.

No longer.

Perhaps our time apart had solidified her intentions, and voicing them aloud and in such an intense, forceful manner couldn't allow her brain or any Earth ideals to stand in the way.

She was ours now. She knew.

We knew it.

We'd been showing her all along. Even through separation, we were still one.

Now we would claim her. Make it official.

She led us to her quarters, a small set of rooms that held no personality. The space was plain and stark. I thought of my residence on Prillon Prime. It was the same way. A place to go between missions. To sleep. Eat. It wasn't a home.

"We will need larger quarters," I said, seeing the bed in the other room. It was small, not meant for a female and her two Prillon mates.

She glanced at the bed, then me. Then Sambor.

"You wish to live here on The Colony?" she asked, her voice soft. The tears were gone, but her eyes were red-rimmed from crying.

Sambor stepped forward, took her hand and raised it to brush his lips over her knuckles. "We will live where you are. It matters not."

Her pink lips parted as she stared up at him. "Your work."

I sliced my hand through the air. "My work is not as important as you. A mate comes first. Everyone knows that—"

"Everyone but Helion," Sambor finished.

"If this is where you wish to reside, we will be pleased to make The Colony our home."

Her hair was wild down her back, far from the sleek styles we'd seen when she was on Prillon Prime. I liked this... natural look of her. The freckles, the curls. The real Lucy.

"I'm only here because of Olivia. It's not where I should be. I didn't know until now where that was. I... I want to live on Prillon Prime. The days I thought... when you were gone"—she swallowed hard—"I realized I had nothing here."

"Olivia and Wulf. The children," Sambor offered.

"It isn't the same as being with you. Prillon Prime is where you both belong. Where I'd like to be. It... fits me."

"My home is not a palace," I shared. I had means and could easily take care of Lucy in a deserving nature, but I was not royalty.

"I want you. *Both* of you. My life's not a Disney princess movie. I don't want a shiny palace."

"Everyone must have something that they're passionate about. Work of some kind. You mentioned your desire for a female... what was the word?" I asked.

"Spa."

I nodded. "Yes, that's it. If it is a dream of yours, it must be fulfilled."

A smile spread across her face and Sambor sighed. I

felt his satisfaction through the collar. I'd made her happy. Thank fuck.

"I would love that, but really, right now I just want to be with you. Both of you."

She stepped into Sambor and placed her hand on his chest. I closed the distance between us and took her other hand.

"Nothing else matters except making my collar turn blue. I... I can't stand it being black. I thought it was going to stay that way forever."

I shook my head. "No, mate. We shall wait no longer. It is my greatest desire—"

"And mine," Sambor cut in.

"—to make you ours."

———

Sambor

ANY CHANCE of a traditional Prillon claiming was long gone the second we crash-landed on that asteroid. Yes, a public claiming was a custom that went back hundreds, if not thousands of years. Formality didn't matter when it came to Lucy. It wasn't important.

All that mattered was that we were together. When the door to Lucy's quarters slid closed behind us, the rest of the universe was left behind. The Hive, my job, Niklas's work was forgotten. All of it would be there tomorrow. Waiting.

Tonight we would make Lucy ours, claim her, turn

the collars to Lorvar blue. It was the only thing I could think of. Lucy, the only thing I saw. The collars made it so that she and Niklas were the only things I felt.

"You understand what a Prillon claiming entails?" I asked, undoing the strap on my thigh holster, laying it and the ion pistol on the table beside me, not taking my eyes off Lucy.

Her tongue darted out, licked her lips. I sensed her eagerness, her arousal.

"You mentioned a little about it when we were at the palace."

Yes, and I'd worked my thumb into that tight ass of hers so she'd know what it would be like.

"We'll both take you," Niklas said, reaching for the hem of Lucy's shirt and lifting it up. She raised her arms to help. When he dropped it to the floor, she was bare from the waist up, her freckled, pale skin reminding me of stars across the galaxy. "I'll be in your pussy."

"I'll be in your ass. I can't wait." She was going to be so snug. *Fuck.*

"Jessica's claiming was broadcast to the entire planet," she said.

I slid a finger along her shoulder and down her arm to her elbow, watched the goose bumps rise. "To Prillon Prime and beyond. To most reaches of the universe, for those Prillons fighting far and wide to know that their Prime had found the perfect mate."

"Our claiming will not be shared," Niklas said. "I do not want to wait."

We hadn't discussed it, but I knew we would not share Lucy with anyone. The sight of her bare skin, the way she responded to us, cried out, surrendered was for us alone. Because our first night together had been at her request, we hadn't followed mating protocol. While I'd gone second, I'd fucked her pussy, which wasn't allowed in traditional Prillon matches until the female became pregnant from her primary mate's seed. Speaking to Niklas, I needed him to know my wishes on the matter now that Lucy would truly be ours. "Now that we are formally claiming our mate, I insist you take the right of the primary male."

Niklas's gaze lifted to mine, shocked, but I knew him better since we'd placed the collars around our necks. Niklas put on a fine show of not caring, but he wanted Lucy, wanted a child with a longing that nearly brought me to my knees. I could wait, had waited. The honor of fathering the firstborn would be Niklas's once our mate was ready. As it should be.

"What does that mean?" Lucy asked.

Niklas was unable to speak, his emotions overcoming his normally eloquent gift for language.

"It means, love, that when you are ready to be a mother, Niklas will be the one to father the child. Until then, I will content myself with fucking your mouth and your beautiful, perfect ass."

"Is that a rule or something?" Lucy asked.

"A tradition," Niklas answered at last. He looked to me. "Thank you, Sambor. I am honored."

I nodded, pleased that Lucy's reaction to being a mother had been joy and excitement. Gods be damned, but these collars would come in handy, help two clueless warriors know exactly what she needed.

"Isn't the public claiming also tradition? You're an ambassador. You represent Prillon Prime," she said, looking at Niklas. "You... you don't want that?"

Having her breasts bare was a distraction. I felt Niklas's need for our mate, and while this conversation was important, I wished he'd kept her shirt on.

Niklas reached out and gently cupped one of her breasts. I watched the pink tip harden as his thumb slid back and forth. "You do not wish to be publicly claimed," he said.

He didn't need to ask, as we could both sense her apprehension to that possibility.

Lucy's eyes fell closed, her head tipping back, which made her breasts thrust out. Two mates, two breasts. I cupped the other.

"I do represent Prillon Prime, yes. What I do with my cock does not. If I wish to claim my mate in private, then the universe will have to come to terms with that."

Her eyes popped open, but they were a little blurry with desire. "But you are important to Prillon Prime. I don't want you to get into trouble. You... you could lose your job!" It was hard for her to talk with us playing. Fuck, she was soft.

"I do not discuss with Prime Nial what I do with my cock."

I couldn't help but laugh at the thought of that conversation.

"My duty is to you," he continued. "Sambor, as my second, has the same responsibility. To satisfy and protect you. Nothing more."

"You'd give up your jobs for me?" Tears filled her eyes.

"We give up nothing. We're adding to our lives. Filling it. Enriching it," I explained. "Without sharing these gorgeous breasts with anyone else. Or any other pink place on your body."

A smile slowly spread across her face; then looked at me. "Dr. Surnen and his second didn't claim their mate publicly."

As they were from The Colony, I was sure she knew their story firsthand.

"You see? It is custom, Lucy, not a requirement." Niklas dropped to his knees before her, his eyes directly in line with her breasts. He leaned forward, put his mouth around one tip and sucked.

She moaned, tucked her fingers in his hair.

When he pulled back, he looked up at her, the nipple wet and shiny. "You are mine. Mine to share with Sambor and him alone."

"Thank God." She nodded. "I'm not sharing you... or your cocks with anyone else. If I wanted to do a livestream porno, I'd have done it on Earth."

I didn't know what a porno was, but I had a good idea of context. I narrowed my eyes, glanced at Niklas. His jaw was clenched tight.

"Anything you do, you do with us. In private," Niklas said. "This porno you desire will be done and seen only by us."

Her eyes widened and she held up a hand, but I felt... exhilaration. "Wait. You want to record it? To save it and... what, watch it later?"

I let my gaze rake over every inch of her nakedness, to think of watching a video record of us loving her, claiming her together, seeing—as many times as we wished—the moment our collars changed color... "Fuck, yes," I growled, whipping off my shirt. My cock was eager to be free of my uniform pants.

"Now?" she questioned, although she knew the answer.

While I sensed Niklas's anger at her being touched, seen or pleasured by another male, the turn of her lips and the lighthearted feeling emanating from Lucy had me cocking my head to the side.

"Now. We shall record the claiming and save it just for us," Niklas said in his deep, diplomatic voice. He stood, scooping Lucy up in his arms as he carried her to her bed, set her upon it. He took off her shoes and socks and worked her black pants down her legs so she was bare.

Niklas growled, waved his hand over her body. "This will not be shared."

I stood beside him, arms crossed over my chest. I didn't have to share my feelings on the topic. She could sense how possessive I was.

She shook her head adamantly, the red curls sliding across the bed. "No sharing. It's just..." She glanced at me, bit her lip. "I know how this is going to be done. I won't be able to see Sam behind me."

"You'll feel me," I vowed. I'd be buried deep in her ass.

She huffed out a laugh, came up on her knees. "I'm sure. But I won't see your face. You won't be able to see mine very well. I want to, well, I don't want to miss any of it. Now. Please."

Niklas was as affected as I was. As primary male, it

was his decision, but he could sense, as did I, that this was something that pleased Lucy. She was aroused by it, the knowledge that either of us could watch her being claimed and fucked... thoroughly.

It was fucking hot. Something I'd never considered or imagined.

Niklas went to the vid screen on the wall, but I stopped paying attention to what he was doing since I kept my eyes fixed on our mate as I stripped.

Lucy licked her lips when I stood bare before her, gripping my cock, stroking it to ease the ache.

"Your skin's like butterscotch candy," she said, looking her fill.

Niklas turned from the vid screen, stripped the rest of his clothes. "And I?"

"Melted chocolate."

"I do not know what either of those items are," I said.

"They're things that are sweet and I like to put in my mouth," she countered, making pre-cum weep from my cock.

I glanced at Niklas, who nodded.

I dropped to my knees on the floor, grabbed Lucy's ankles and tugged her toward me, settling her legs over my shoulders. Before me was her wet, eager pussy. "I've got something sweet that I want to get my mouth on."

I didn't say anything else, just licked her pussy from top to bottom. She gasped and I gripped her thighs to keep her in place.

Niklas moved to sit by the head of the bed, cupping and playing with her breasts. "This is being recorded,

Lucy. Do you like knowing we'll be able to watch later how Sambor pleasures you with his mouth?"

She moaned and I felt her need to come through the collars. I'd get her there. It was my newest mission and one I would not fail.

———

Lucy

OH. My. God.

I'd thought the two nights we'd had together had been hot. But this? They were here. With me. Touching me. *Licking* me.

They weren't dead. Far from it. I could feel their touch, but I sensed them. The collars ensured I knew they were close, that they were right here with me. Physically and mentally.

I had never once considered the idea of filming sex. With Nik and Sam it was different. There were no games. This was real. Every bit of it. They'd meant it that day Nik brought the collars. Every word, every action had been true.

They wanted me.

I wanted them. I wanted it recorded and saved for posterity. I wasn't going to show it to my grandkids, but I had a feeling it would keep all of us hot for years.

I squeezed my knees against the sides of Sam's head. He was so good with his mouth. My clit was worked with his tongue with such precision that I was already close to coming. Their need built up my need, and when he slid a finger inside me and curled, I bucked into the air and came.

Hard. I was lost to it, and when I finally caught my breath, I wasn't sure if I'd smothered Sam with my pussy.

With gentle hands, he lifted my legs from his shoulders, kissed an ankle. His lips and chin glistened with my arousal. Nik pulled me up and onto his lap.

Kissed me, his tongue finding mine. I was sated and yet still craved. I felt their need and knew we were far from done. He didn't lift his head, only shifted so I straddled his waist.

"Please," I whispered, looking into his dark eyes. "I feel your ache. I want to ease it."

"The only way is for me to sink into you," he said, his voice deep and husky with desire.

I nodded as he brushed my hair back. Shimmying my hips, I settled myself over his hard cock and worked myself onto it. He was big. So big that it took a little time to get him all in. When I was finally seated once again on his thighs, I sighed.

"Yes," I breathed. I needed to be filled. To have him inside me. I was lost without it. But now I would have him, *them,* forever.

Glancing over my shoulder, I looked to Sam. "Now, Sam. I want you, too."

He didn't require any more urging. Patience had been the driving force of him watching and waiting. Nik was inside me, but even though he was huge, it wasn't enough. I wanted Sam, too.

I had no idea where it had come from, but he held up a small container.

"This will ensure you are ready."

"What is it?" I asked the question, but I wasn't really listening to the answer. I was too busy shifting my hips, grinding on Nik. And I had to know he was alive and safe and mine.

"Lubricant." Sam's response barely registered, and I realized just how much I trusted these two. My warriors. My mates.

I focused on that feeling, the way I loved being with them, how safe I felt. How beautiful and perfect and wanted.

Sam groaned as he bent over and claimed my mouth. "I can feel you loving me, mate."

I smiled at him, then turned to Nik. "I love you, too, you know."

"Gods, yes." Nik's hands came to my waist, distracting me as our emotions spiraled out of control. He lifted and lowered me, his cock waking up all kinds of special places inside me. I gasped when something hard nudged my back entrance, and I felt the lube fill me. Directly after, Sam's hand settled on my lower back, his thumb pressing against my entrance.

I met Nik's eyes. Watched him as Sam began to slowly work the lube into me, taking his time to prep me and stretch me some. I knew he'd be bigger than his thumb, and I appreciated the effort.

It also felt so good.

Sweat dotted Nik's dark brow, and as his fingers

clenched on my waist, I knew he was holding off. Keeping me still while staying so deep.

"She's ready," Sam said as his thumb slipped from me.

I couldn't hold still any longer but rode Nik, working myself on him. "Nik!" I cried, close to coming again. His hips lifted to fill me as much as possible.

Sam's hand settled on my shoulder, and I slowed, then stopped.

"Time to make you ours," Sam said.

Nik looked over my shoulder at Sam and nodded.

Nik lifted his hand to cup my jaw. "Do you accept my claim, mate? Do you give yourself to me and my second freely, or do you wish to choose another primary male?"

The intensity of the moment, their anticipation of my response, nearly drove me over the edge. "What am I supposed to say?"

"Fuck. Just say yes." Sam's lips traced the line of my spine, his kisses moving up and down my back.

"Yes. Hell, yes."

I was shocked to feel Nik's relief and cupped his face.

"Without doubt or reservation, I want you both. Do you hear me?"

He nodded and I kissed him, wiped the suspicious hint of a tear from the corner of his eye. Kissed him again.

I felt Sam's growing need to join us, to become one with us. "Fuck, Niklas. She said yes."

Nik chuckled, kissed me hard and fast. "Then we claim you in the rite of naming. You are mine, and I shall kill any other warrior who dares to touch you."

Sam moved behind me, his lips brushing my ear. "You

are mine as well. To love. To pleasure. To fuck. To protect. To adore and touch and need."

I thrilled at their words, at the solemn tone of their emotions. This was more than a marriage. This was forever, a physical and psychic bond with two of the most amazing warriors I'd ever known.

Nik placed his hands on my hips and pulled me a bit forward, parting my ass cheeks open just enough for me to gasp. "Fuck her, Sambor. Make her ours."

I imagined what was next, the heat of being surrounded, filled to bursting, coming as I rode both their cocks.

My pussy clenched. I threw my head back, and the sound that escaped my throat was not one I'd ever heard before.

"Fuck, she's going to come just from your words," Sam said, settling himself behind me, a hand on my hip.

"Yes, claim me," I breathed. "Do it. God, do it now."

Nik hooked my neck and pulled me down for a kiss, which arched my back, thrust my butt up for Sam.

Nik kept kissing me as Sam pressed against me, stroked my back and, while taking his time, insistently pressed into me. My body was no match for an eager male, and he breached my virgin ass with a silent pop.

I gasped against Nik's mouth. He watched my face as Sam slowly and carefully worked himself inside.

"Fuck, she's so tight. Perfect," Sam said, his voice almost a snarl. With that, he spanked me. His hand came down on my upturned ass. Not hard but with some sting. It lit me up, got me wet. Made me moan.

"Breathe, mate. Good. We're going to fuck you

together. You're going to come. I can feel it through the collars. I'm not going to last, you're so fucking perfect. We're going to fill you with our seed and then the collars will change to blue. You'll be ours."

"Yes," I whispered.

Nik thrust up into me. Sam retreated.

"Oh!" I cried. My eyes fell closed, and I reveled in the feel. Bit my lip at the strange sting, the intensity too much. It wasn't painful but uncomfortable. Yet it felt so good. I knew both my guys were in me. I was connecting us, making us one. Their need, their desire, how good they felt came through the collars, and I couldn't last. I didn't want to. It was like an avalanche of feelings, building and sliding and overpowering.

I screamed my release, milking both their cocks. My nails dug into Nik's shoulders, keeping myself anchored as if I would fly away.

Impossible, with both of them holding me.

Nik groaned, thrust up. Came, hot pulses of his seed filling my pussy. Sam didn't last more than a few seconds longer, our orgasms leading to his.

I blinked my eyes open, looked to Nik. He was smiling, and I couldn't help but offer a weary smile in return.

My gaze dropped to the collar about his neck, admired the brilliant, deep blue. I touched mine but couldn't see it. "Did it work? Is it blue?" I needed to know. I didn't want that damn thing to be black a moment longer.

"Mine," Nik said.

Sam was still deep inside me, and he kissed my bare

back. Brushing my hair forward and over one shoulder, he stroked along the back of my collar.

"Mine," he repeated.

I was theirs. I knew it. Felt it. Nothing was going to change that. We'd proved that our love endured the worst nightmare imaginable. We'd survived.

We'd live happily ever after. Maybe I did have a fairy-tale life after all.

I rubbed the collar around my neck with a smile and spoke one word that was the absolute truth, about both of them. Forever.

"Mine."

A SPECIAL THANK YOU TO MY READERS...

Want more? I've got **hidden** bonus content on my web site *exclusively* for those on my mailing list.

If you are already on my email list, you don't need to do a thing! Simply scroll to the bottom of my newsletter emails and click on the *super-secret* link.

Not a member? What are you waiting for? In addition to ALL of my bonus content (great new stuff will be added regularly) you will be the first to hear about my newest release the second it hits the stores—AND you will get a free book as a special welcome gift.

Sign up now! http://freescifiromance.com

FIND YOUR INTERSTELLAR MATCH!

YOUR mate is out there. Take the test today and discover your perfect match. Are you ready for a sexy alien mate (or two)?

VOLUNTEER NOW!

interstellarbridesprogram.com

DO YOU LOVE AUDIOBOOKS?

Grace Goodwin's books are now available as audiobooks...everywhere.

LET'S TALK!

Interested in joining my **Sci-Fi Squad**? Meet new like-minded sci-fi romance fanatics and chat with Grace! Get excerpts, cover reveals and sneak peeks before anyone else. Be part of a private Facebook group that shares pictures and fun news! Join here:

https://www.facebook.com/groups/scifisquad/

Want to talk about Grace Goodwin books with others? Join the **SPOILER ROOM** and spoil away! Your GG BFFs are waiting! (And so is Grace) Join here:

https://www.facebook.com/groups/ggspoilerroom/

GET A FREE BOOK!

JOIN MY MAILING LIST TO BE THE FIRST TO KNOW OF NEW RELEASES, FREE BOOKS, SPECIAL PRICES AND OTHER AUTHOR GIVEAWAYS.

http://freescifiromance.com

ALSO BY GRACE GOODWIN

Ascension Saga, book 3

Trinity: Ascension Saga - Volume 1

Ascension Saga, book 4

Ascension Saga, book 5

Ascension Saga, book 6

Faith: Ascension Saga - Volume 2

Ascension Saga, book 7

Ascension Saga, book 8

Ascension Saga, book 9

Destiny: Ascension Saga - Volume 3

Other Books

Their Conquered Bride

Wild Wolf Claiming: A Howl's Romance

ABOUT GRACE

Grace Goodwin is a USA Today and international best-selling author of Sci-Fi and Paranormal romance with more than one million books sold. Grace's titles are available worldwide in multiple languages in ebook, print and audio formats. Two best friends, one left-brained, the other right-brained, make up the award winning writing duo that is Grace Goodwin. They are both mothers, escape room enthusiasts, avid readers and intrepid defenders of their preferred beverages. (There may or may not be an ongoing tea vs. coffee war occurring during their daily communications.) Grace loves to hear from readers! All of Grace's books can be read as sexy, stand-alone adventures. But be careful, she likes her heroes hot and her love scenes hotter. You have been warned...

www.gracegoodwin.com
gracegoodwinauthor@gmail.com

Printed in Great Britain
by Amazon